BONES BY THE FOREST ROAD

A VIKING WITCH MYSTERY

CATE MARTIN

Cover design by Shezaad Sudar.

Rune art by BettyStrange at Dreamstime.com.

Ratatoskr Press logo by Aidan Vincent Kise.

ISBN 978-1-951439-86-6

❀ Formatted with Vellum

CHAPTER ONE

IT HADN'T BEEN SO VERY LONG since I had last seen Villmark. Only a few days. But when I arrived there that mid-April morning with Nilda and Kara by my side, everything just felt different. Not like I was seeing it for the first time. More like I was seeing it with new eyes.

Part of it was the weather. I had moved to the North Shore in September and had survived my first Villmark winter. I had also seen some fine days with lots of sun and blue skies, but never one so warm as this.

After being covered in mounds of snow for months and months, everything looked wide-open now. The shutters were down from the windows, and the streets were wider without the snowbanks taking up so much space.

But those were all good things. I should be looking at Villmark and seeing a happy place, because it was.

And yet, I was uneasy. And I couldn't quite put my finger on why.

It seemed like everyone in Villmark was outside, soaking it all up. April wasn't too late in the year for another snowstorm to blow through, and we all knew it. But for the moment, anyway, it was warm enough for short sleeves. I was wearing a T-shirt myself. I had a flannel shirt tied around my waist in case the temperature plunged while walking through the woods. But just now the warm sun on my skin felt so good, I didn't even mind how winter-pale my arms were compared to the Mikkelsen sisters beside me.

They were both as tanned as ever. How did they manage that? They had spent the last few months working long shifts in a literal cave, guarding the ancestral fire that protects all of Villmark.

The only bigger mystery was where they found time for all the working out they had to do to maintain their top-level physique. I wasn't overweight at all, but my pale arms looked downright flabby next to their sculpted musculature.

The three of us reached the well at the center of town to find even more crowds gathered there. Meat was cooking on grills set up all over the commons, even though it was hours until lunchtime. The smell of sizzling beef filled the air, punched up a notch every time drops of fat set the flames hissing and roaring.

And I could hear voices everywhere, people chatting in their gardens, shopkeepers calling out to each other as they set up their outdoor tables on the sides of the main street.

But what must have been the fourth cluster of children washed up the cobblestone street to us, breaking around the three of us like river water around jutting rocks, then fell back together again behind us to carry on shrieking towards the edge of the woods.

That. That was what felt different about Villmark to me this time. Everything around me was absolutely bucolic, and yet I was on edge.

And I was feeling a particular fear for the children so close to the woods.

"They're completely safe, Ingrid," Nilda said to me, reading my mind.

"Not completely," I said, my grandmother's words still too fresh for me to push them aside.

"It's a rare thing, any of them disappearing," Kara said. "Nora only knew of three, and they were spread out over centuries."

"Three that she knew returned," I reminded her. "There were more that just... disappeared."

"Maybe we can do something about that," Nilda said. "But we have another mission first."

"Yes," Kara said emphatically.

"What mission is this?"

I knew that voice before I had even pinpointed where it was coming from. Directly behind me, of course. All winter long, I had seen him under-dressed everywhere. Tromping through snow in inadequate shoes and no coat or hat. I had only just learned the reason for this: that he had a power to move from one doorway to another in some random location he seldom got to choose. He was never dressed correctly because he never knew where he was going, or when the door would lead him outside.

So it was a bit of a change to see him looking overdressed for once. But not in a way that suggested he had been pulled into the center of town unprepared. Really, he looked like any other dedicated goth, dressed all in black with sleeves down past his wrists and a collar buttoned all the way up his throat. Soaking in the sun was clearly not for him. But his pale look worked with his dark hair and eyes. He was a perfect goth.

"Hello, Loke," I said.

"We're going to find the Thors and bring them home," Kara said.

Loke raised his eyebrows. "Not a small mission, then."

"Or an easy one," Nilda agreed. "Ingrid, you have to go see Haraldr before we leave town, right?"

"Yes," I said. "I don't imagine that will take long, but I can't put it off."

"I know," Nilda said. "How about Kara and I pick up all the supplies we need, and then we'll meet you where the road back to the cabin starts at the edge of the woods?"

"If you don't mind doing all the shopping, that sounds perfect to me," I said.

"It's not a problem. Noon?" she said.

"Noon," I agreed. Then she and Kara disappeared into the throngs of people milling through the marketplace.

"Come on," Loke said. "I'll show you the back way to Haraldr's place."

"Through a magic doorway?" I asked.

"I was thinking of going a couple of blocks over, away from the main roads," he said. "I try to avoid magic doorways."

"You could probably avoid them better if you were avoiding talking to my grandmother less," I said pointedly.

He didn't answer, but I hadn't expected him to. He would ask for help in his own time, and nothing I did would change that.

Not that I was going to stop bringing it up, of course.

"Did you get some news that has you running to Thorbjorn?" he asked me as we strolled past walled garden after walled garden. I could hear brooms sweeping away the remains of last year's leaves in a yard or two, but there were fewer voices here.

"Kara had a vision," I said.

"Kara did?" he repeated. But then he shook his head as if he wasn't surprised. "Anything specific?"

"Just that they're in danger. But my grandmother said we should go find them," I said.

"That's probably a good idea," Loke said. He glanced around as if to be sure we weren't overheard, but we were alone on the quiet street. "I know it looks like a happy scene today, but something has me on edge."

"So it's not just me," I said. "I thought it was because my grandmother was telling us about children going missing from the village."

"Missing?" Loke asked.

"Not currently. She just meant like Leifr, who left years ago but is back now. And also Odd Oddsen," I said.

I didn't have to explain those two to Loke. The two of us had been talking with Leifr ourselves when it became clear that he had been born much further in the past than his visible age would indicate. He had gotten lost in the woods outside of Villmark, in places where time moved differently than it did closer to the shore of Lake Superior.

And everyone in Villmark had known Odd, the man who claimed

he had been among the original settlers from Norway, which would make him centuries old. He hadn't claimed to be Odin himself, but he liked to heavily imply it. I still had a hard time parsing out what was real about him and what was just story.

"There was also another woman, a friend of my grandmother's, by the name of Reginleif," I said.

"Don't know her," Loke said.

I found that a bit surprising. I had just assumed that Loke knew everyone. Not just in Villmark. He spent more time in the modern world, in the fishing village of Runde, than any other Villmarker save my own grandmother.

He also had a lot more experience in the wilds to the north and west of Villmark. Those directions led not to the woods of northern Minnesota, but back through time and space through magic I didn't remotely understand.

I had once walked on a road that led to distant mountains, mountains I had been told were actually in Old Norway. Not the Norway of today, but the Norway that had existed when my ancestress Torfa had first created this place.

I had also passed through an area that had reminded me strongly of Iceland, although I had never been there before. I was starting to get the feeling that going deep enough into the wilds would take you to all sorts of places.

But the wilds were called that for a reason. I had encountered many strange creatures out there, some friendly, but many definitely not. And I knew there were other things out there I had yet to face. Things like giants.

What were Nilda, Kara and I about to walk into? Were we going to find ourselves in over our heads?

I pushed that thought from my mind. "Tell me what you're sensing in Villmark," I asked Loke.

He shrugged. "Just a feeling. Like a storm is coming. Although obviously not that," he said, gesturing at the cloudless blue sky hanging over us. "I don't know what it is. But I don't think it's just us.

Not that I've talked to anyone about it. But if you walk around town, you'll see a few of the more sensitive souls who are sharing our disquiet. Mostly, I'm thinking everyone would rest easier if the Thors were back."

"It's been too long with no news," I agreed. The Thors had gone out on patrols before. It was their self-appointed job, after all. But never before had all five of them gone out at once, for so long, with no word sent back.

"You're leaving at once?" he asked.

"After I talk to Haraldr," I said. "My grandmother is drawing us a map to guide us. Not that we know exactly where they are. But that friend of hers I mentioned, Reginleif, she knows the roads of the north better than almost anyone, I gather. She's as old as Odd was, maybe older."

I touched the pendant I wore around my neck, the one that was in the shape of a spear. It had been a gift from Reginleif to my grandmother years ago. It was how I would prove who I was. Because as much as Reginleif would likely be an ally in our cause, "friendly" might not be the best way to describe her. From what my grandmother had told me, I gathered she preferred to wander the wilds alone.

"Mjolner is going with you?" Loke asked.

"If he wants to," I said. Mjolner was more independent-minded than the average cat. He could also travel vast distances in an instant, although how he did this I had never seen. If he didn't want to stay with me, there was nothing I could do to keep him.

But whenever I needed him, he was always there. If he chose to stay with my grandmother, I would still have his protection. I had no fears on that score.

"Do you want to come with us?" I offered.

"As much as I love spending time with you and the Mikkelsen sisters, I'll have to decline," he said. We had nearly reached Haraldr's house on the south end of town, and Loke was already bearing further west, towards the road that would lead him to his home nestled between a couple of dairy farms.

"Are you sure?" I asked. "We could really use your help."

He gave me a grin, but it was dimmer than his usual. "I bet," he said. "But alas, I really have to stay here."

"Is Esja all right?" I asked. His sister would be the only thing that would compel him to stay, or to do anything at all. Especially if she was feeling sickly again.

"She's doing well," he said, but I could tell that, as usual, that wasn't the full story. But he just pointed to Haraldr's front door. "You have to get going. Much to do. Esja and I will be fine. Please don't worry about us even for a minute. You'll have enough to deal with, I'm sure, being in the north."

"I'll think of you both anyway," I said.

He laughed and nodded. "Have it your way. But if you do get yourself into trouble, have Mjolner come get me. I can be there in a jiffy, provided you're somewhere with a door."

"I gather that Reginleif travels in a wagon," I said. "I don't know if it has a door."

"I'm sure if it comes up, you'll think of something," he said. "I trust when I see you again, you'll have Thorbjorn hovering over you. It'll be like old times."

"I certainly hope so," I said.

He waved, then headed off downhill towards the rolling, cow-dotted hills beyond the edge of town.

Then I heard children laughing again, in the distance. A perfectly happy sound that once more sent a shiver up my spine.

Was I doing the right thing? Was it wise for me to leave Villmark? My grandmother may still be the volva of Villmark, one in a long line of witches charged with protecting the descendants of those who our ancestress Torfa had brought here from Norway, but it was a responsibility we were sharing now.

Especially since I had discovered that she had been overtaxing her magic for years. She was doing better now, but she still wasn't back to her full powers as a volva.

And she was still in the cabin a half-day's walk to the north. So far away, if anything here should go wrong.

But, no. Loke was right. The best thing I could do for Villmark was to get the five Valkisson brothers back, the Thors.

And while I wouldn't characterize it as "hovering," I wanted Thorbjorn back at my side.

Whatever I was sensing about Villmark, I could face it as resident volva far more bravely with my loyal guardian with me.

CHAPTER TWO

I KNOCKED on Haraldr's door, or started to anyway. It swung open almost at once, leaving my hand tapping on nothing. I had to look down to make eye contact with Fulla, Haraldr's assistant and general helper. She was only twelve or thirteen, and was no family relation to Haraldr so far as I knew, but he relied on her for everything.

"He's expecting you," she told me, then turned to lead the way down the long central corridor, her thick blonde braids swaying ever so slightly behind her as she walked. I left my boots on the mat, very aware of every mud puddle I had tromped through on my walk through the woods, then jogged to catch up.

I caught up with Fulla just as she reached the door to the library. She knocked once, briskly, then opened the door and waved me through.

Haraldr was sitting in a chair close to a crackling fire. He and Fulla must be the only people in Villmark not enjoying the day outside.

"Are you feeling all right, Haraldr?" I asked as I joined him by the, frankly, too hot fire. He had a wool blanket tucked all around his bony legs. A book rested on his lap, as if he had just shut it when Fulla had knocked, but something about the mussiness of his remaining halo of silver hair over his bald head told me he had been resting his head against the wing of his chair. Napping.

"Well enough, well enough," he told me. But he didn't get up from his chair as he usually did. "Your time is short, I take it?"

"You know what I'm up to?" I asked as I sat down in the chair across from his. He nodded. "Kara is anxious to start. In truth, so am I. But if there is a reason to linger, I will do so," I told him.

"No, you and Kara should listen to your instincts," he said.

"Loke and I were talking, and we both sense something building. Do you know what I mean?" I asked him.

He shrugged. "I am not as sensitive to such things as you, you know. I am merely your inadequate teacher in arts which I do not practice myself."

"Nonsense," I said. "You've taught me more than I can say already. And we have so very far still to go."

"Such a look in your eyes today," he chided me. "I'm not going anywhere. I will remain your teacher in the lore of the runes until we reach the final rune."

Then he opened the book on his lap, only lifting the front cover to pick up a card he had left tucked in there. He glanced at it as if to verify it was correct, then held it out for me to take.

I looked at the shape, like an R drawn with only straight lines, no curves.

"This one is very appropriate for what you're about to do," he told me.

"How so?" I asked. I knew it sounded like an R, and with it we were nearly done spelling out the word futhark, the word that gave the rune alphabet its name. But that was all.

"Its name is reidh," Haraldr told me, folding his hands over the now closed book on his lap. "And it is the rune of journeys. But more than that. It is traveling through time and space. It touches on how we measure time and space."

"And I'm going into the north," I said, nodding, "where time and space are simply not the same as they are here."

"Just so," Haraldr said, touching the side of his nose and winking at me. "Isn't it funny how the world works out?"

"I'll laugh about it later," I said. Not that I couldn't see the irony. I was just still so worried about… everything. "If this rune means journey, and I'm on a journey, am I going to have a harder time telling when I'm seeing this rune for a reason, or when I'm just seeing it because I have it on my mind?"

"Interesting question," he said. "You'll have to take care. And don't neglect your meditation practices. I know you'll be with friends. That has made you lax in the past."

"I'll make the time to meditate on this every night," I promised. But he wasn't wrong. I had promised him that before, with other runes. "I know my trouble with the ase rune was because I let Odd Oddsen get into my head."

"This might give you trouble for a similar reason," he warned me. "This is a rune of dance and music, of poetry in all its forms."

"Ugh," I said, looking down at the drawing on the card like it had already betrayed me.

"You are a visual artist. That will always be your strength. But you should at least be able to access if not appreciate some of the others," Haraldr said.

"I suppose I should be studying the poetry," I sighed. I glanced around at the frightening number of books around us.

"When you get back," he told me. Which was suspiciously close to exactly what I wanted to hear.

"Are you sure?" I asked.

"I'm not loaning you any of *my* books. Not with where you're going," he said with a sniff.

"Fair enough," I said.

"There is one other thing that troubles me," he said, fidgeting in his chair ever so slightly. Like he had debated even bringing it up, and now that he had, he wasn't sure it had been the right decision.

"About poetry?" I asked.

"About reidh," he said. "It deals with journeys, yes, but it also deals with justice."

"I've dealt in justice before," I said. It was almost all I did, since coming to Villmark. How many murders had I investigated? How many perpetrators had I brought to justice?

"It also deals with harmony," he said. It still sounded like he was fighting against every word, only reluctantly getting them out.

"You don't think I'm harmonious?" I asked. Only half-joking. He was clearly worried about something.

"It deals with the harmony between an individual and the society they are a part of. Finding that balance," he said. He was moving his hands as if weighing invisible objects.

"I get it," I said. "How am I going to tap into that when I'm so far from home?"

"That is my fear, yes," he said, resting his hands on the book once more.

"If I were here, would you be worried about what society I was harmonizing with? Villmark or Runde?" I asked.

"It is… interesting that this comes up when you are going where you're going," he hedged.

I chewed at my lip. "I'll always belong to both. Wherever I choose to live, whatever I choose as my calling, that will always be true."

"Certainly, you've made that clear," he said.

I looked down at the card in my hand again, then tucked it away in my art bag. "The way you talk about this rune coming up now with all that's happening, it's almost like you're talking about fate," I said. "Is that a thing?"

"It depends on what you mean by fate," he said. "It's a very large topic, too large to address now. And I've only scratched the surface of what it all means myself, after a lifetime of study."

I looked around at all those books again. If I started reading them, it would be all I would be doing for years. Decades, even.

"What I've found with the matter of fate is much like what the two of us have discovered with our work together with the runes," he said.

"What's that?" I asked.

"Book learning is enlightening, and not to be scoffed at. But living the truth of things is where the real wisdom is," he said.

"I'm not sure I follow that," I admitted.

"I could tell you everything every philosopher has ever had to say on the topic of fate, destiny, free will, and all that. But it's all just words without a deeper meaning until you feel those forces yourself in your own life," he said. Then he gave me a sad sort of smile. "Please don't be angry when I say this, as I was angry when my own tutor said it to me, but you are young yet. You've seen only a little of the road of life. I know you won't see things as I do. I ask only a little indulgence when an old man tells you that the longer his life goes on, the more it feels like it has its own structure. None of it was clear at the time, but now that I draw closer to the end of things, I can see how it all flows like a story. And this rune, at this time, to me feels like just the next page in that very long book."

I nodded, but didn't look up at him. I was pretty sure I wasn't going to be any good at hiding my distress. Not at his words about fate. In truth, I still didn't quite follow what he was telling me there.

But he kept talking about things coming to an end. I had no idea how old he was. Younger than my grandmother, I was sure, but my grandmother was far, far older than she looked. Being a volva changed things for her, and maybe for me too. But every time I saw Haraldr, he looked measurably older. And more frail.

And I had so much left to learn.

"Go on your quest. I promise you everything else will sort itself out," he said, smoothing the blanket over his knees. "I will be stronger when summer is here for real. Please, don't worry about me."

That was the second person telling me not to worry while I was gone. It was… worrying.

"Ingrid," he said, and I realized my inattention had not slipped his notice. I looked up at him, then noticed I was still chewing at a thumbnail and dropped my hand. "It is important for all of us here in Villmark that you succeed. We need the Thors."

"I will do my best," I promised.

It sounded so small in my ears, but he beamed at me brightly, and a little of the Haraldr I had first known was back in his eyes. "That will surely more than suffice. Now, excuse me not walking you to the door."

"Don't even worry about it," I said, leaning over his chair to kiss him on the cheek. He flushed at the attention and waved for me to leave him alone with his book.

I caught a glimpse of the title as I left. I had expected some weighty tome of dreadful knowledge. About fate or destiny or the nature of time.

But he was reading a leather-bound copy of *The Complete Adventures of Sherlock Holmes*.

Not what I expected.

I was still smiling to myself about that when I reached the far northern edge of town. Nilda and Kara were already there, three heavy packs resting on the ground beside them.

"Did you say all your goodbyes?" Kara asked me as she helped me get one of the packs on my back. It was a modern hiking backpack with a little cushioned pad where it rested against the small of my back and wide straps that settled comfortably on my shoulders.

I could just tell already how grateful I was going to be each night when we stopped to camp and I could take this thing off.

But I also knew the time would come when the lightness of the pack would be the most worrying thing. What if our supplies ran out before we got back?

I was so not ready for this kind of journey.

But Nilda and Kara were both bright-eyed, excited for the coming adventure.

I realized I hadn't answered her question yet, and wracked my brain. "Who would I say goodbye to?" I wondered.

"I suppose there was no time to go down to Runde," Nilda said, and I felt a stab of guilty shame. I had forgotten my Runde friends entirely. Again.

"No, no time," I said. "I didn't see Roarr either, although I'm sure Loke will tell him what's going on."

"We ran into him," Nilda said, and Kara nodded.

"He wanted to come with us," she said.

"You said no?" I asked. Then felt guilty again for inviting Loke along without asking them first.

"I know what you're thinking. The three of us against whatever is out there, we're going to need all the help we can get," Nilda said. Ever practical.

"But we're also leaving Valki alone to tend the ancestral fire," Kara said. "Leaving Roarr here to help him out felt like the better plan."

"Yes, I think you're right," I said. "Loke is here too, but with his sister, he can't really be relied on in that way."

"If Villmark is in danger, he will stand up for it," Kara said.

"We've done all we can here. The best thing now is to get the Thors and get home again as quickly as we can," Nilda said.

So we set off, back the way we'd come just that morning. We had one last goodbye to make, to my grandmother. Then we'd really be on our way.

If only I could convince myself I was making the right decision. Villmark, vanishing in the distance behind me, was still making me feel so on edge.

But I had to get back before I found out why.

CHAPTER THREE

IT WAS late afternoon before we were once more crossing the narrow promontory that divided the main shoreline from the rocky outcropping that Frór's cabin was built on. The day was still warm, but the breeze off of Lake Superior was chill, and I finally wanted that flannel shirt I had been wearing around my waist all day.

Of course, I couldn't put it on without taking the pack off first. And I would need help to do that.

I was *so* not ready for this kind of journey.

As we drew closer to the cabin, I was surprised to see my grandmother wasn't sitting outside, waiting for us. My black cat Mjolner was outside, but I wouldn't call sprawling out in a patch of setting sun waiting for us. Particularly as he didn't even bother to lift his head as we walked past.

I opened the door and called, "Mormor?"

"In here!" she called back. Kara helped me get the pack off, and then I unlaced and pulled off my hiking boots. Only then did I follow my grandmother's voice to the corner of the main room where my easel and art supplies were set up.

"What are you doing?" I asked as I came around the easel.

"Finishing up your map," she said, leaning in to make a few final strokes. Her tongue was just visible, poking out from between her teeth as she concentrated.

When I had first come up to Runde from St. Paul, I had been following one of my grandmother's hand-drawn maps. At the time I had marveled at the details, how the waves on the shore she had drawn had seemed to wash in and out despite being only ink on paper.

I knew now that had been a magical map. Most people drove past Runde without noticing it at all, tucked in under one of the highway bridges as it was. I myself had driven past it before I finally consulted that map rather than the GPS on my phone.

But the map I was looking at now put that map to shame.

First of all, it was huge. She had taken a page from one of the largest of my art pads, the one that was two feet by three feet of heavy paper. I seldom worked that large myself.

But my grandmother had filled the entire space. Every inch of it was covered in intricate details. Trees, rivers, grass, waterfalls. Everything.

Not only did it seem to be moving, I was sure if I looked at it more closely with a magnifying glass, I would see even more details than I did now.

"That's all I can remember," my grandmother said. She sounded regretful. Which was crazy.

"This is amazing," I said, and Nilda and Kara hurried over to lean over our shoulders and murmur their agreement.

"I used to be a bit of an artist myself," my grandmother said, blushing pinkly. "I didn't stick with it. But I still remember a thing or two."

"You did this in pen," I said, leaning closer to peer at those strokes. "And you didn't sketch it in pencil first."

"No, there wasn't enough time," she said. She sounded disappointed in herself. Like she should've done more. On my busiest, most caffeine-fueled days, I had never done so much in so little time.

And I had only done it with slightly better technique. After years in art school.

"Ingrid, are you all right, dear?" she asked me, which only made me feel guiltier.

But it wasn't jealousy I was struggling with. Not really.

I struggled to find the words for what the problem was. Nilda nudged her sister, and they both sneaked off to the kitchen. But the two of them being there wasn't what had my tongue so tied.

"It just needs a minute for the ink to dry, then I'll roll it up for you," my grandmother told me. She checked that every ink pen she had used was capped correctly, then put them back exactly where she had found them. "I didn't think you'd mind if I used your things."

"No, of course I don't mind," I assured her.

She spun the stool around to face me. "What is it, then? Are you worried about Thorbjorn?"

"Of course," I said.

"But that's not all of it," she said, folding her arms.

"No, I'm worried about me," I admitted. "I don't know that I'm up for this. Whatever has happened to the Thors, how am I going to fight that? I'm no warrior. And I've barely learned any magic yet. So I'm no witch either."

"You'll do what you've always done," she said. "Your best. And that's got the job done every time."

"So far," I grudgingly admitted. "But the three of us going, it's leaving people in Villmark in a lurch, isn't it?"

"I'm here, aren't I?" she asked.

"Here, not in Villmark," I said.

"I see your point, but we'll all be fine," she said. She touched a few spots on the paper and, finding it dry, stood up to start rolling it up tightly.

"I wish I could be in two places at once," I said.

"Not even Mjolner can do that. Although he gets pretty close," she said, then handed me the rolled-up map. "You three need to get going."

"It's so late already—" I started to say.

"You can't wait for morning," my grandmother interrupted me. "You need to get moving and keep moving. That was the one feeling that struck me again and again as I drew this map. Urgency. So much urgency."

"My feeling in Villmark is that I'm leaving it exposed to something," I said.

She pressed a finger to her lips as she considered this. "I suppose you are. But you can't stay. Villmark needs the Thors back."

"Maybe someone else should go," I said, as much as I hated to say it.

"No one is going to find those boys faster than you and Kara. And Nilda, of course, but her motivation is... different," my grandmother said with a mischievous gleam to her eye.

"Mormor, I'm being really serious here," I said.

"I am too," she insisted, but that gleam was still there. "It has to be you three. I don't know why, but it does. And it has to be now. So, come on! I'll walk with you as far as the crossroads."

My feet really didn't want to get back into those boots, but they weren't the ones making the decisions. Then Kara helped me back into the pack, which hadn't gotten any lighter since I had set it down.

"Here," my grandmother said, shoving her best walking stick towards me.

"I can't," I said.

"But you will," she insisted, thrusting it at me again. I tucked the map into the strap of my pack, then took the stick from her.

It felt good in my hand. Like the wood was meant to nestle in my palm. "Is there magic in this?" I asked suspiciously.

"There's magic in everything," she sniffed. She took another walking stick from the box near the door, then waved for the three of us to head out the door.

As we crossed the grassy field in front of the house, Mjolner sat up with a wide cat yawn, then trotted after me, falling into step beside me like a trained hunting dog.

We were halfway to the crossroads before I realized the stick in my grandmother's hands wasn't one of her spares that she kept for guests. It was the twisted staff that Odd had brought with him when he'd first come to our house. Just before he died.

I had thought it had been placed in the cairn with him.

I would ask my grandmother if it was magic, if I wasn't sure I would get the same dismissive answer as before.

"Here is where we part," my grandmother said, a formal tone to her voice as we all stopped at the crossroads. I looked south, towards Villmark, although that was too far away and beyond too much forest for me to see a hint of it.

Then I deliberately turned to the north and planted my grandmother's walking stick one pace ahead.

It was like something flowed up from the earth, up through that staff, up into my hand. I felt energized. Not quite up to this task, maybe, but definitely capable of walking for a few more hours.

I turned back to my grandmother, but I could tell by the smile in her eyes that she knew exactly what I was feeling.

"Safe travels, Nilda Mikkelsen," she said, and pulled Nilda down to plant a kiss on her forehead.

"Safe travels, Kara Mikkelsen," she said. She kissed Kara's forehead, too, but then she whispered something, something only Kara could hear.

Kara flushed, but only nodded as she stepped back from my grandmother's embrace.

And now she was looking at me. "Safe travels, Ingrid Torfudottir," she said and placed a kiss on my forehead.

It was like the walking stick, times a thousand. Warmth and strength flowed through me at her touch.

Definitely magic.

"Look after them all, Mjolner," she said, but didn't attempt to kiss the cat. He made a murmuring sort of meow, his attention already fixed to the north.

"Go on, all of you," my grandmother said. Then all the merry warmth left her voice as she added, "and don't look back."

We walked shoulder to shoulder along the path, Mjolner at my heels. There was a forest to the north, but it was almost out of sight from the crossroads. It was so hard, walking on to that distant point, never looking back.

I felt like she stayed there, watching us go, Odd's staff in her hands. But I couldn't know for sure.

Then we were in the woods, and with enough trees behind us, the pressure to look back or not look back lifted. We walked on without a word as the sun sank ever lower in the west.

I didn't realize that I was leading the way until Nilda said, "are you sure we're heading the right way?"

I stopped and looked around. I knew this place. I had been here once before with Loke. We were very close to where we had found the wyldmen. They were friendly enough, but staying the night amongst them would be taxing. Their conversational skills were rudimentary, to say the least.

"I was just going north," I admitted. "This road follows the lake."

"But we have to get away from the lake to get to Old Norway," Kara said, and gestured for me to take out the map.

I slid it out of the strap of my pack, then unrolled it. It was dark under the growing spring foliage of the trees, but the map seemed to glow softly with its own light.

"We're meant to go towards the mountains," Nilda said, pointing out where we were in the very bottom, far right of the map. Then she pointed to where the mountains sat on the map, at the very opposite corner.

"So many things between," Kara said.

"We're going towards the mountains, but our destination is wher-ever Reginleif is, right?" I said. "It's not so very far. Isn't that her, there?" I pointed to a wagon tucked under some trees. It was only about a third of the way across the page.

I had no idea how far that was, though. Reidh might govern the measures of time and space, but my grandmother had left us no clues.

"Trolls, wolves, wyldmen, giants. It's all between us and where we're going," Nilda said.

"Wyldmen aren't so bad," I said. "For that matter, neither were the trolls." I had encountered a band of them on one of my first adven-tures with Thorbjorn. They had fought the Thors, but only because someone else had put them up to it. They had stopped, and had treated me with complete respect even though I could barely call myself a volva now, let alone then.

"You've been around more than we have," Nilda said. "Let's just take a moment and reaffirm what we're doing. Are we sure we want to do this?"

"I'm sure," Kara said at once. Then she gave Ingrid a quick glance. "I think Ingrid is too. Only you have no personal stake in this, Nilda. Are *you* sure?"

"What do you mean, I have no personal stake in this?" Nilda asked. "Like I'd let my only sister face all this without me! Is there a bigger personal stake than that?"

"Kind of?" Kara said. Nilda scowled at her, but Kara just laughed. "Your day will come, sister. For now, I'm glad to have you here with me."

"Me, too," I said. "Both of you. There's nothing out here that the three of us can't handle. We know that's true, or my grandmother would never have let us go."

"That's true," Nilda said. "Still, I'll feel better once we find this Reginleif person."

I couldn't argue with that.

I put the map away, and Nilda pointed out the smudge on the horizon that was all we could see of the mountains of Old Norway. Then I gripped my walking stick, put the thoughts of the wyldmen in their little village out of my mind, and took the first step off familiar roads and into the unknown.

CHAPTER FOUR

THE THREE OF us walked until it was too dark to see. Then we camped under the trees, woke in the gray light of dawn, and walked all day until dark again.

We did this for four days, and those mountains never seemed to get any closer. We didn't encounter anything on my grandmother's map either. We just kept walking through the forest. Sometimes we followed a narrow track, barely a furrow in the ground. Sometimes it was a path worn smooth by countless feet. And sometimes it was a wide road with two grooves worn deep a wagon-span apart.

It would change from track to road to path and back again at random, and nothing about the forest around us gave any clue as to why some places looked more travelled than others.

I had a hunch we were traveling through time somehow. But the weather stayed a steady warm spring, and the growth on the trees matched that season. So my theory was probably not quite right.

Then, on the fifth day, we woke to find rain pattering softly on the leaves of the trees around us. It was a gentle rain with no real wind, but with the sun behind the clouds, the air got colder.

Nilda and Kara were dressed in Villmarker clothes, just like they always did save for their visits to Runde. They seemed comfortable enough once they'd draped cloaks over themselves and their packs and drew their hoods up to keep out the rain.

But I was wearing modern clothes. Jeans aren't the most comfortable thing when they get wet, and they clung to me coldly as we walked. But my hiking boots were sturdy, and I didn't slip even as the road turned to a slick mud. And my rain jacket kept my top half dry, although I had to wear my pack outside of it, and I wished my hood was as deep as the Mikkelsen sisters'.

It had to be about noon. Not that I could tell by the sun, which didn't even give a hint as to its location behind those dark gray clouds. But my stomach was starting to rumble.

Then I realized part of that wasn't just hunger from a long morning's walk. I could smell sausages cooking over an open fire.

"Look," Nilda said, pointing ahead of us. The path had morphed into a road again, but now we'd finally found one of the wagons that had worn those ruts so deeply. It was sitting motionless in the middle of the road, its wheels resting in those muddy grooves.

The wagon definitely wasn't something from modern Minnesota. Even without the ox yoked to the front of it, the design was from another age. And yet it wasn't Nordic either. It was all of wood and looked like a cylinder lying on its side over the wheels. The roof curved all the way around, and the circular back was dominated by a single door with a little window set into it. The window had a shutter which was closed, so I couldn't see inside.

It looked to me like the sort of wagons the travelers used in Ireland. And yet the knot motifs worked around the door and window were pure Nordic, not Celtic.

"Isn't anybody here?" Kara whispered. She and Nilda both had their swords out, and they crept up to either side of the wagon, looking all around them carefully.

There was a campfire on the side of the road beside the front of the wagon, but there was no sign of anyone tending it. And yet those sausages, while sizzling, were not burnt. Someone must have been here a moment ago. But where did they go?

"Is this Reginleif's wagon or a trap?" Nilda asked me. I unrolled my grandmother's map and found the drawing of the wagon on it.

"I think it's hers, but where is she?" I wondered. "Fetching more firewood?"

We all jumped at a sudden laugh that rang out from behind us. But it wasn't the cackle of a foe, just a merry sound that somehow made the fire shine brighter through the rain.

"So cautious, all of you!" the woman behind us said in clear Villmarker Norse. She did indeed have an armful of dry wood. She was wearing a cloak much like Nilda's and Kara's, and the hood was drawn up so that her face was in shadow. But I could see her blue eyes laughing out at me from within the depths of the hood.

"Reginleif?" I guessed, fingering the pendant around my neck.

"Indeed. Good to see you, Mjolner," she said to my cat as she passed the three of us to dump her wood near the fire. Then she dusted off her hands.

Mjolner meowed, then hopped up onto the narrow step at the bottom of the wagon's door and began washing the rain off his fur.

Nilda and Kara looked to me for guidance, but if Mjolner felt safe, I was sure there was no reason to worry. I gestured for them to put their swords away, and they did so. Then we approached the fire where Reginleif was poking at a cast-iron pot set among the embers. When she lifted the lid, the smell of roasted carrots and turnips filled the air.

"My grandmother sent us to you. Nora Torfudottir?" I said.

"Yes, I saw your pendant, Ingrid Torfudottir," she said. Then she sat back on her heels and smiled up at all of us, pushing her hood back only enough so that we could see her face. Her skin was finely wrinkled, and yet there was something still youthful about her. Perhaps that was the effect of her merrily dancing eyes. "I've made lunch for you all. I'm sure you've been munching jerky and dried fruit while on the move for days now, and I thought you'd appreciate a little change of pace."

"We were anxious to get to you," I said.

"And now you've reached me, and you can take a little break," she said. "Sit. Eat."

Nilda and Kara exchanged a shrug, then settled onto two of the flattish rocks near the fire. I opted for the stump of a tree that jutted out of the ground between the campfire and the road itself.

Then Reginleif loaded up plates with sausages, vegetables, and generous dollops of a spicy, grainy mustard.

As hungry as I was, it was a lot of food. We all ate without speaking until we were stuffed, then picked at what remained on our plates.

"I know Ingrid, but I don't know you two," Reginleif said to the Mikkelsens.

"I'm Nilda Mikkelsen, and this is my sister Kara," Nilda said. "We share a quest with Ingrid."

"A quest?" Reginleif said, sounding impressed.

"We've never met, so how is it you know me?" I asked. "Through my grandmother?"

"No, through Mjolner," Reginleif said. "Everyone knows Mjolner. And he's very fond of you."

Great. So now I'd met yet another person who could talk with my cat. I was starting to feel a little left out that he never spoke to me in anything besides meows.

"We're looking for the protectors of Villmark," Kara said to Reginleif. "The five brothers who are the sons of Valki. We call them the Thors."

"I'm sorry. I know nothing that will help you on your quest," Reginleif said, and my heart sank.

We had walked so far for nothing?

But she wasn't done talking. "But I am on my way to the Dísablót. You should join me. There will be others there, travelers in the north. Someone there will know something that will help you. It's this evening, but we have plenty of time to reach it. We're practically there already."

"The Dísablót?" I asked.

"Different places celebrate it in different ways," Reginleif said. "But those of us who haunt the north—those of us travelers who are women, I should say—like to gather in the spring and just remember the goddesses together. Feasting and dancing under the stars. It's a nice little party. And you're certainly welcome to join us. You are now travelers of the north, too, after all."

Kara puffed up a little, liking this description of us. I wasn't sure we were quite in the same league as the others, and certainly not with the Thors, but I said nothing.

"It's a shame about the rain," Nilda said.

"Oh, that will stop soon," Reginleif said with complete certainty. "The stars will come out when it's time for the dancing."

"It does sound like fun," Nilda said to Kara and me.

"And if someone there knows where we can find the Thors, it's the best lead we have," Kara said.

"I'm for it, too," I said. "If it comes to nothing, we've only lost a day. We can always go back to just aiming for the mountains."

"That's not the way to find your friends," Reginleif said. "Things here don't work the way you're used to."

"What do you mean?" I asked.

"You can't get to a place by aiming for it, for one thing," she said. "The mountains will always be there, on the horizon. They never get any closer or any further away. They are part of what defines this place. A boundary, but not in the physical sense."

"So, if we wanted to get there, how would we do it?" I asked.

Reginleif sat back on her rock and tapped her chin thoughtfully. "If I could put it into words, it wouldn't guide you."

Nilda tipped her hooded head away from the fire, so I was pretty sure that Reginleif didn't see her rolling her eyes. But Kara was looking at Reginleif intently, a studious look to her face, like she was trying to puzzle a meaning out of those words.

"What do you recommend, then?" I asked.

Reginleif grinned at me. "Only what I've already told you. Come with me to the Dísablót. Meet the other women gathered there. After a night of feasting and dancing and chatting together, I think you'll start soaking up some of what you need to know."

"It's a thing to be experienced and not merely learned?" I said, thinking of the things Haraldr had said to me.

"Exactly!" Reginleif said, pleased. "Now, let's douse this fire and get that old ox moving. We want to be there before sunset so you can see the valley before it gets dark."

Nilda and Kara dealt with the fire while I helped Reginleif wash the plates, pot and pan in a pail of water she had fetched from the back of her wagon.

Once they were as dry as we could get them while the rain was still dripping down on everything, Reginleif stacked them all together, then put them in my hands.

"Just set them in the obvious place inside the wagon if you would, dear," she said, and turned her attention to the ox, who was calming chewing something, not bothered at all by standing out in the rain.

I climbed up into the wagon and blinked for a moment, letting my eyes adjust to the darkness.

A bed was tucked against the front wall, and Mjolner was curled up on its pillow, fast asleep. Over the bed was a high row of cabinets that reminded me suddenly and with a surprising pang of my own bed back in Runde.

But that bed was gone now. A magical tornado had destroyed my grandmother's cabin on the river. The bed I had slept in there, both as a young girl and just a few months ago when I had moved north, it was all gone now.

I took a deep breath and pushed that feeling of loss away, then looked around the wagon again. There was a little table with two even smaller stools between me and the bed. With the long, blue cloth over the table reaching down to the floor, it reminded me of nothing so much as a fortuneteller's table. It lacked only a crystal ball.

Then I looked to the right and saw another cabinet built into that wall. One of the doors stood open, and I saw a few more plates on the bottom shelf, the two shelves above it currently bare. I put the pan on the top shelf, the pot in the middle, and stacked the clean plates on top of the others. Then I shut the door and hopped back out of the wagon.

It was a cozily small space, but it felt like a home. Mjolner certainly acted like he belonged there. I didn't think the itinerant life would ever appeal to me, but I could see that it suited Reginleif perfectly.

And I wondered just who I was about to meet in a few hours. Would they be hikers like the three of us had been, or would they all have wagons like Reginleif?

"Everyone ready?" Reginleif called from the driver's seat on the front of the wagon.

"We're set," Nilda said. Then Reginleif made a clicking sound with her tongue and the ox leaned into the yoke. It took a bit of effort to get the wagon moving, but once the wheels pulled free from where they had settled into the mud, it rolled along nicely. The three of us had no trouble keeping up with that ox's plodding pace.

I pushed my hood back from my eyes, just for a minute, looking to the north. I could still see the darker gray of the mountains stark against the lighter gray of the clouds.

Reginleif must be right, because those mountains looked no closer than they had when we had left the lake shore behind days before.

But I felt like we were getting closer. And I wished with all my heart there was a way to tell Thorbjorn that.

That I was closer. That I was on my way.

That I would see him soon.

CHAPTER FIVE

By late afternoon, those mountains still didn't look any closer, but we were definitely in taller hills than before. I almost wanted to call them foothills. They certainly felt like they were building up to something, each hill taller than the one before.

And finally, it stopped raining. The clouds began to break apart, and the birds in the trees started singing again.

The sun was low in the west when we finally left the forest behind. The road continued on, snaking between two steep hills that were all broken rock and scrubby grass. We followed it with the wagon as it snaked again the other way, winding between ever steeper hills.

It was almost like we were in a canyon now. I could probably climb the hills around us, but I wouldn't want to try it if I didn't have to. They were so steep I'd need hand and feet together to get up them, and the effort would be more than I had left in me after yet another long day's hike.

Then suddenly the hills in front of us parted, opening up into a wide meadow inside a sort of box canyon. The hills on the far three sides were taller and steeper even than the ones behind us.

And from the center of each poured a magnificent waterfall. None of them were so wide as the waterfall back in Runde, the one that hid the entrance to the world of Villmark, but they were all taller. And the blue water that fell from those heights looked cold and clear, like glacial runoff. They fell down onto moss-covered rocks, forming little pools.

But no river or stream ran away from any of them. It was like those pools were hiding drains that just carried the water away, out of sight.

The sound of the falling water echoed through the canyon, as did the calls of the birds who hunted the fish as they tumbled over the falls.

But I could also hear the sounds of women's voices, and I tore my eyes away from the waterfalls to where the road ended at the base of an immense tree. It stood alone in the very heart of the meadow, spreading its branches wide as if to protect all below it.

And gathered around that tree was a cluster of tents and another wagon much like Reginleif's.

"It looks like a small crowd this year," Reginleif said as we walked up to the gathering. "Last year, there were more than a dozen of us. But this year, the roads are different. Harder to follow."

"So it's not just us who can't get where we most want to go?" Kara asked her.

Reginleif smiled fondly down at her. "No, it's not. It's all of us, to a greater or lesser extent. But I know someone here can help you."

"If everyone here travels the north, they might know where the Thors are already," I said hopefully.

Before Reginleif could answer, the door at the back of the other wagon banged open and an immense woman jumped out onto the grass. She was tall enough to play professional basketball, but so broad in the shoulders she looked like she'd be better suited to football. She appeared to be in her forties, her reddish-blonde hair threaded with only a few silver strands that almost looked like decorative touches, the way they brought out the pattern of the plaits of her braids.

She was dressed in well-worn leather pants with patches at the knees and seat, and her boots were spattered with mud. She wore a hand-knit sweater that, like her pants, had seen better days, unraveling at the cuffs and with a sizable hole in one sleeve at the elbow. And as she drew closer and raised a hand in welcome, I thought the glow in her green eyes was almost as merry as the sparkle in Reginleif's.

"Well met, strangers!" she said, then laughed at herself. "Well, strangers and Reginleif. It's been an age, Reg, hasn't it?" Her Norse was just barely intelligible to me, her accent thick and strange.

"It's been a year, anyway," Reginleif said in her pitch perfect Villmarker Norse. She pulled her wagon up next to the other, then hopped down with surprising dexterity for a woman of her age. Whatever age that actually was. I knew she had been born centuries ago, but I had no clue how many years her body had seen.

"Thorfinna, this is Ingrid Torfudottir and her companions Nilda and Kara Mikkelsen," Reginleif said as she unyoked the ox, then left it to wander on its own with a fond slap on its rump.

Thorfinna. The name fit her. There was no family resemblance in the face, but her size made her the equal of any of the Thors I knew.

"Ingrid Torfudottir. Relation of Nora?" Thorfinna asked, the smile gone from her face as she looked me over closely. But at least she had taken Reginleif's hint and switched to our variant of Norse.

"That's correct," I said. "Nora is my grandmother." My fingers were twisting that spear pendant around and around, but that was only a token for Reginleif. It was no sign to Thorfinna that I was worthy of her trust.

"Odd Oddsen was going south to see Nora. Do you know anything about that?" she asked me.

I desperately tried to read her expression, but it was closed off. She wasn't giving me any hint what answer she expected or desired. But I could tell from her posture as she waited that she wasn't going to let me go without giving her one.

"I'm sorry to be the bearer of bad news, but Odd Oddsen is dead," I said.

"Dead," she repeated, her tone flat.

"Yes. Murder, I'm afraid. But the guilty party was dealt with, and my grandmother and I erected a cairn for Odd near the shores of Lake

Superior. It's tall enough to be seen far out over the water, by those who know what to look for," I said.

Thorfinna said nothing for a long time, just looked at me with her thick arms folded over her even thicker chest. Then she sucked at her teeth and said, "never liked him, myself. I'm not sorry to hear he's gone. But I know he was important to the people of Villmark. So I guess it would be the kind thing to offer condolences."

"In truth, he was no friend of mine either," I admitted.

That seemed to be what Thorfinna was waiting to hear. She didn't exactly break into a grin, but her expression lost its stoniness. She said, "I confess, I've never met your grandmother, Nora. But I know her by reputation. You and your friends are quite welcome here."

"Thank you," Nilda said warmly, and Kara murmured the same.

"What brings you three to the north? I'm guessing it wasn't the Dísablót. The women of Villmark used to range this far to celebrate with us, but that all petered out decades ago. Or maybe centuries. I don't get into the villages enough to know how time is passing."

"We're looking for the protectors of our town. The five sons of Valki," Kara said.

"The Thors, you mean," Thorfinna said with a laugh. "Yes, I know them. They are hard to miss, even in a place like this."

"Are you from Villmark originally?" I asked her. Maybe she *was* related to them, just from a branch much further down the family tree.

But she was shaking her head. "No, no. And I seldom go so far south as that. But your boys, on occasion, range far enough north and west for our paths to cross. I confess, I feel a bit protective of them. Like they're all my little brothers. I look out for them when I sense them near. But no, I'm not from Villmark. I'm from what your people call Old Norway. I came across the mountains quite by mistake, who knows how many years ago, and I've been here ever since. No desire to go back."

"Have you seen the Thors lately?" Kara asked her.

Thorfinna sucked her teeth loudly. "I'm afraid I have."

"Afraid?" I said.

"Was something wrong?" Kara said at the same time.

"I don't rightly know," Thorfinna said. "I didn't approach them. I usually don't. Mostly, they never know I'm there, and I prefer it that way. But the last time I saw them, there was something strange about the way they were walking. It was like they were under some sort of spell."

"How long ago was this?" Kara asked.

"Oh, I really can't say," Thorfinna said with another short laugh. "Spend enough time in the north, and you'll know what I mean."

"What sort of spell?" I asked.

She frowned at me. "That I really, *really* can't say. Not my area of expertise at all. It was just a sense I got, that something wasn't right."

Kara and I exchanged a look. This was not good news. And there were so many unknowns. What could we even do with this information?

Except for worry over it. Which we were doing enough of already.

"You know who *does* spend time in the Villmark area?" Thorfinna said suddenly, clapping one hand on my shoulder and the other on Kara's and propelling us both to where another woman knelt on a spread-out linen sheet sorting out dried plants. "Yngvildr. I know I couldn't tell you anything useful to you, but she might. Yngvildr!"

The woman kneeling on the sheet looked up, a sprig of dried flowers in each hand. She looked startled at the sound of her name, but I couldn't blame her. Thorfinna had a trumpeting bellow of a voice.

"Yes?" she said, setting the flowers aside and wiping her hands on a long apron as she smoothly rose to her feet. She was dressed like many of the women I saw in the marketplace in Villmark, in a long sheathe-like dress with a full-sized apron tied around her waist. Her clothes showed better care than Thorfinna's, with only a hint of a single mending at the front hem of her skirt done with neat, almost invisible stitches. But whatever color had once dyed the fabric was muted to a ghostly gray by innumerable washings.

She shared that ageless look that Reginleif had, but I guessed she was younger than Reginleif and older than Thorfinna. Her blonde hair had turned more silver than Thorfinna's had.

"Yngvildr, this is Ingrid Torfudottir, Kara Mikkelsen, and..." Thorfinna broke off, looking around until she caught sight of Nilda jogging to catch up with the rest of us. Something had caught her attention, but there was no time to ask what it was now. "Ah, yes. Nilda Mikkelsen."

"Well met," Yngvildr said as she nodded at each of us in turn. Her Villmarker Norse was clearer than Thorfinna's, more practiced.

"Ingrid is Nora's granddaughter," Thorfinna said, and gave me a little push closer to Yngvildr.

"Oh, Nora!" Yngvildr said fondly.

But before she could say more, Thorfinna leaned in to whisper loudly, "Ingrid tells me Odd has been murdered. No loss, am I right?"

"Well, it certainly is a loss," Yngvildr said, her cheeks flushing. "A murder? That is always a subtraction from the society of people, is it not?"

"You don't fool me, Yngvildr," Thorfinna said. She was backing away, wagging her finger admonishingly at Yngvildr while walking backwards to where two other women were building a bonfire well away from the tree. "You hated Odd as much as anyone. You might as well admit it!"

Then she turned and walked more briskly towards the pile of wood.

Yngvildr laughed nervously, her cheeks flaming red. But then she bobbed her head. "It's true. I never cared for Odd. But I'm not the sort to gloat over the death of another."

"No, I get that," I said as diplomatically as I could. I guessed her feelings about Odd's death were as mixed as mine. It would be terrible to say so out loud, but in my heart of hearts, I felt like life in Villmark was surely lightened by his no longer being around to meddle in it.

Yngvildr went on, "I won't claim to know your grandmother well, but she has been a great help to me many times in the past. I owe her so much. If there's anything I can do for you while you're in the north, please just ask."

"There *is* something," Kara said, looking at me.

"We're looking for the Thors," I said. "You know who they are?"

"I do," Yngvildr said warmly.

"When did you see them last?" I asked, dreading an answer as vague as the one Thorfinna had given me.

"Let's see," she said, clicking her tongue and looking up as if consulting the skies. "Yes, it was shortly after Jule. After the Wild Hunt stopped running amuck. I assumed they had something to do with that."

"That was more Ingrid's work," Kara said, and Yngvildr's eyes widened.

"And my grandmother's," I quickly amended. Then, before Kara could argue, I pressed on. "Did you notice anything strange about them?"

"Well, they were all going out on patrol at once. That was certainly strange," she said.

"Did they look like someone had cast a spell on them?" I asked.

"A spell!" she said, as if it was the most shocking thing she had ever heard. "No, I didn't notice anything at all like that. Not at all. They were talking and laughing and being boisterous men, like always. I stayed clear of their path, as is my wont, but from a distance they seemed quite fine."

"At least we have a better sense of the time," Kara said.

"Only it doesn't tell us more than we already knew," I said glumly. "We were there when they headed out just after Jule. I was hoping for some more recent knowledge."

"I'm sorry, my dears," Yngvildr said. But then her face brightened again. "But if you're curious about spells, it's really Hulda you'll be wanting to talk to. She knows a bit about that sort of thing. Nothing like your grandmother, but this far north, she would be the authority."

"Is Hulda here?" I asked.

"She's right over there gathering wood for the fire," Yngvildr said, pointing to a woman that would normally be considered statuesque if not for being in such close proximity to Thorfinna.

"Thank you," I said, and Kara and I crossed the grassy field to where Hulda was picking up sticks that had fallen from the massive tree. Nilda trailed along behind us.

Hulda saw us approaching and straightened up, pressing a hand to her back. In one instant, I saw a woman in her mid-fifties trying to massage out a cramp from too much stooping. Then I blinked, and she was a woman in her twenties, hand resting just over the curve of her buttock as she thrust out her ample bosom.

I blinked again, hard, and the older version was back again. But this was no comfort.

That effect reminded me entirely too much of Halldis. Halldis had used that skill to trick men into doing her bidding. But there were no men here. So what was Hulda up to?

For that matter, what was with the curve-hugging outfit? Even the older version of her looked dressed to draw every male gaze up and down those curves and spiral in to the seemingly bottomless chasm of her cleavage. Was that really just what she was comfortable wearing?

"Well met, Villmarker women," she said as we drew close enough for conversation. "Thorfinna told me who you all were."

"And why we're here?" I asked.

She raised her eyes as if in surprise. "Not for the Dísablót then?"

"Not just," Nilda said. I saw she was resting her hand on the hilt of her sword. It looked casual, and yet I knew she didn't normally stand that way. So I wasn't the only one whom Hulda was rubbing the wrong way.

"Oh, right. The Thors," she said, then bent to pick up another stick and add it to the pile in the crook of her left arm. "I knew they were in the north. We all sense when they come so far from home."

"Do you know where they are or what happened to them?" I asked.

I didn't want to ask about the magic. Not her. If she had been more like Yngvildr, I absolutely would have. But this woman felt too much like everything she said and did was a performance. And we would never know if what she said was truthful, or just what she wanted us to hear.

I caught Kara's eye, and she gave me the smallest of nods. We were on the same page.

"No, I'm afraid I can't help you there," she said. She strolled a few steps, then bent to pick up another stick. That bundle in her arms was really quite scanty. She was not very efficient with this work. At all.

Then she pinned her green eyes on mine, and I could see a different sort of laughter there than Thorfinna and Reginleif had in theirs. This was a mocking sort of merriment. "Tell me, Ingrid Torfudottir, was Frór with them?"

"I think you know he was," I said.

She laughed. "You are correct. Yngvildr mentioned it to me," she said. Then she laughed again, a sound that was starting to grate on me. "Not because you asked, of course! She was just talking to you. When would she have found the time? No, she mentioned it to me when we met here a few hours ago. Frór is—how can I say this?— something like a pet of mine."

"Yeah, you probably wanted to pick a different word there," Kara grumbled, but Hulda pretended not to hear.

"I don't know your grandmother, I admit, but if she wanted to put any sort of claim on that man, she had years and years to do it in," Hulda said, giving me another one of her greenly gleaming looks. "I guess she was never worth sticking around for. But Frór and I have had some good times."

"And yet he spends as much time in the south as he does in the north," Nilda said. I had no idea what she was driving at. Hulda gave her a puzzled look as well. Nilda smirked ever so slightly and said, "so I guess *you* had nothing worth sticking around for either. By your own logic, of course."

"Of course," Hulda said, but with dripping disdain. "Well, if you'll excuse me, I simply must get this wood to the fire."

She flounced away. Kara and I were just catching Nilda's hands to squee over the excellent point she had just made when Hulda spun back around to stab an accusing finger straight at me.

"And the murder of Odd Oddsen was a very bad omen. Very rad! Someone will pay for that in the end. Perhaps an entire village of someones. Mark my words."

Then she flounced away again.

"She was pleasant," Kara deadpanned.

I was about to ask the other two whether Hulda reminded them of Halldis too, when suddenly there was a fourth person standing in our little huddle.

I thought it was a woman, under all those hoods. The hands and feet that were visible were so bony there was barely any flesh, just gray wrinkles of skin stretched over protruding joints. The rest of the body was nothing but layers of once-fine fabric, now nothing but tatters that danced in a breeze I didn't feel.

I could see a face under the layers of hood, but it was genderless. Their eyebrows were nearly gone, as was the hair on their head. Only a few silver wisps covered a grayish scalp scarred with sunspots and aggressive-looking moles.

Then their bluish-white eyes widened. I wasn't sure if they could even see me. That looked like very late stage cataracts to me. But then their gaze fixed on me, and I felt absolutely pinned down.

"Odd Oddsen should not be dead," the ragged remains of a woman's voice said, her accent thick. "No, no, no. Should not."

"We brought the murderers to justice," I said. "There was nothing more we could do."

"He was buried with all honors," Nilda added.

"Surely he fights on in Odin's hall of fallen warriors," Kara said.

The woman just shrieked. It didn't really feel like a response to anything we had said. More like she had a need to do that periodically, and we had been talking to her at the appointed time.

Then she looked at me again, and I flinched away from that too-intense gaze.

"I have seen the Thors," she said, leveling a bony finger first at me and then at Kara. "I have seen them."

"Where?" we asked as one.

"In the webs. Caught in the webs," she said. "All the spiders say so. All of them."

"Okay?" I said uncertainly.

"The spiders," she repeated, as if I was just not understanding her.

Then she said, "the spiders are upset about Odd. You really ought to tend to the spiders. They need to know life will go on without Odd."

I started to say okay again, but she wasn't done.

"Life go on without Odd? Not the same! Not the same! Oh, this is a bad omen. Very bad. Very, very bad."

Then she just turned and walked away from us.

"I see you met Njorun," Reginleif said from behind us, causing all three of us to jump again.

"Is she always like that?" I asked, sweeping my hands to where Njorun was disappearing into the shadows of the tree.

"Oh, yes," Reginleif said, nodding gravely. "Yes, Njorun is the wisest woman I know. I hope you marked her words well."

I turned to look at Kara to make sure I wasn't going crazy. But Kara was just gaping at Reginleif. She glanced over at me and shrugged.

Nothing that old woman had said had made the least bit of sense.

"Well, come along," Reginleif said to us. "The bonfire is going now, and the feasting begins."

I don't think I had met five stranger women in my life. And now I was going to sit down and eat with them.

At least dancing like lunatics under the moon and stars would feel like the natural thing to do in their company.

CHAPTER SIX

THE PART about feasting among the descendants of Vikings that I had forgotten was the mead.

I had tried to avoid it at first, wanting to keep my head clear. Not that I had any illusions about meditating later. I had managed it every night of the journey so far, without anything that felt like a resulting bond with the reidh rune, but even I knew there was no meditating in the middle of an all-night party. I just wanted to be alert in case any of these strange women would say something actually useful about the Thors.

But Thorfinna wasn't letting me get away with not drinking. And from the first sip, I knew this was not my grandmother's mead. It hit me hard, and it demanded more.

The rosy light of dawn had never hurt before, but when I opened my eyes the next morning, it was like stabbing jolts of pain straight to my brain.

I sat up with a groan, and Mjolner, sleeping on the pillow beside me, gave me a low meow of sympathy.

I was in my sleeping bag close to the side of Reginleif's wagon. I had no memory of getting there. I had a few memories of dancing, though, which had me blushing in embarrassment.

I was suddenly very, very glad I couldn't remember much about the night before. It was clearly better that way.

I rubbed at my head, wondering if Yngvildr had any herbs in her stores that were good for hangovers. Probably. But I doubted she was awake yet. I had a vague sense that, as much of a night as I had made of it, I had still been the first to turn in.

I decided that, at the very least, I could find a drink of water. Reginleif had a barrel of it tied to the back step of her wagon. I got up and stretched, belatedly noticing Nilda and Kara sprawled out nearby. They were on their sleeping bags, but still dressed, and those bags were still rolled up tightly.

They were going to feel even worse than I did when they woke.

I pulled on my boots, then stumbled around to the back of the wagon. The water was there, cold and faintly sweet, and I drank a few handfuls.

Then I noticed that the wagon door was standing ajar. I nudged it further open and saw Reginleif's bed, empty and unslept-in.

I wondered where she had slept. Wherever she had finally collapsed after all the dancing, I guessed.

But Mjolner was beside me now, and the meowing he was doing sounded concerned.

"What is it?" I whispered to him. I was pretty sure I was the only one awake so far. Except possibly Njorun, who hadn't eaten or drunk anything the night before, just sat staring into the flames of the bonfire. She might be awake, but I definitely didn't want to attract her attention.

Mjolner was lifting his nose, sniffing at the air. He made another mournful meow, then looked up at me with his yellowish-green eyes.

"Trouble," I said. Not a question. I didn't smell anything, but something was definitely wrong. I could feel all the little hairs on my neck rising up. "Which way?"

Mjolner sniffed the air again, then walked off through the tufts of spring grass. I followed behind. The ground looked flat from a distance, but once off the road, I realized it was actually quite irregular, rolling up and down in clumps that was rather exhausting to walk across. It was like the ground itself wanted to trip you.

The grass became ever taller as we walked, occasionally dotted with the first flowers of spring. But Mjolner slipped through as easily as a snake through the grass. I had to push the tall blades aside and part the larger clumps to follow.

Then we reached a sort of clearing where the grass was flattened. It almost looked like we had been dancing here, but this was nowhere near where we had built our bonfire.

And at the heart of that spiral of flattened grass was a pair of tall, smooth stones. They looked like the sort of stone that made up the hills around us, but the arrangement was far from natural. It had the feeling of a holy site, an impossibly old one whose meaning had been lost to time.

I was moving closer, hand outstretched to touch those stones, when Mjolner meowed again, insistently. I looked down to see what he was getting all worked up about.

And saw Reginleif sprawled across that flattened spiral of grass on the far side of the stones. Her hand was outstretched, much like mine still was. Like we were reaching to each other. Or both of us for the stones that stood between us.

But I knew at once that the hand I was looking at was lifeless.

I came around the stones to kneel by her side and saw what I had missed on the far side of the stones.

They were covered in blood. Not like it had been poured from above, more like a hand had smeared blood over the face of them again and again.

I looked again at Reginleif's hand. Yes, her palm was not only stained, the cup of it held a congealing reddish-brown pool.

I sat back on my heels and felt like crying.

Why did this keep happening to me? It was like I attracted murders. Even out in the middle of nowhere, they found me.

Then I *was* crying, because although I had only known her for a day, I knew that Reginleif hadn't deserved this. And she had left enough of a mark on me on the hours I had known her that I felt an emptiness in my heart.

But some of it was probably the hangover. I was a mess.

I rubbed the tears from my eyes and face, then looked at the scene before me again.

I had a job. It wasn't the job I had come up here to do, and it was killing me that this was going to delay my mission to find Thorbjorn and his brothers.

But that didn't change the fact that this *was* my job. I had to figure out who had done this, and how and why it had happened. And I had to make sure that justice was done, one way or another.

I knew Nilda and Kara would help me, but at the moment I was pretty sure what they needed most was more sleep. And no one was going anywhere, not this early in the morning. I rather doubted anyone else would even start stirring until much closer to noon.

In the meantime, I should start sketching the scene. See what I could learn. Because all I saw now was a woman who had smeared a bit of blood on a stone, and had a bit more in her hand, but no other sign of an injury.

And adding it all up, I didn't think I saw enough blood loss to kill anyone. Even someone as old as Reginleif.

Or maybe I should say, *especially* someone as old as Reginleif. There was nothing natural about her time span. What would it take to kill someone of her apparent power?

I had a brief vision, a fragment of the night before, all of us dancing under the stars. We had all had our own glows, some brighter than others, some different, darker colors, but every last one of us had had a glow.

And Reginleif's glow had been golden happiness. And so bright.

I stood up, intending to walk back to the camp to get my art bag, and nearly collided with Njorun, who had been standing silently right behind me.

I felt a belated shiver up my spine at the thought of her hovering there without me knowing. Mjolner hadn't even given me a clue.

Then suddenly, Njorun was screaming.

I always thought the word "bloodcurdling" was just a metaphor. But I felt it happening as that scream went on and on.

And I saw it. That pool of blood in Reginleif's extended palm curdled right before my eyes.

I wanted to throw up. And that wasn't just the hangover talking.

I put my hands over my ears and waited for Njorun to run out of breath.

She had to. Sooner or later.

Right?

CHAPTER SEVEN

Njorun screamed on and on.

I had been wrong about the needing to take a breath thing.

Then Mjolner started yowling in protest. My first thought was that was all I needed. Competitive caterwauling.

But then Njorun fell silent, bowing her head. As if the cat had shamed her into being quiet.

For a long, pleasant moment, the only sound was the whispering of the breeze through the spring grass. Then I heard voices approaching.

"I was going to show you yesterday. It was just over here—" I heard Nilda saying. Then she and Kara burst into view.

At first, their relief was palpable. They had found the source of that screaming, a now quiet Njorun. And they saw I was there as well. I could tell they thought I had stopped the screaming, and were thankful I had gotten there first.

But even as I watched their faces, I could see the rest of the scene finally sink in to their awareness. The stones, the blood, the body.

"You were here yesterday?" I said as I stood up and brushed bits of the ground off the knees of my jeans.

"When you two were taking with Yngvildr, I noticed this place in the grass," Nilda said. She was speaking softly, like we were in a church. I had the same feeling about the space, and that feeling had returned after Njorun had stopped screaming.

Kara was looking at Njorun uncertainly. Her first instinct when dealing with such obvious grief was to offer comfort. But I could tell that didn't feel like the right response to Kara when dealing with Njorun. The old woman barely seemed human. She certainly didn't seem like someone looking for a hug.

"What is all the fuss about?" Thorfinna demanded as she charged into the clearing. She, too, saw Reginleif's body and stopped so suddenly that Yngvildr behind her collided into her immoveable form, stumbling back into the grass. But Hulda caught her elbow, holding her until she had her balance back. Then they drew closer, still arm in arm, and stood over Reginleif with the rest of us.

"Mjolner and I found her here," I told them all. "But she's been dead for some time."

No one said a word. I looked from face to face, hoping for some hint of who the culprit might be. We were the only ones in the valley that I knew of. And everyone had stayed up later than I had. I felt pretty safe in crossing Nilda and Kara off the list of suspects. But the others I had no clue about.

"Does anyone know what this means, what she was doing?" I asked, pointing at the blood on the stones. "Is this part of the Dísablót?"

"I've never seen her do anything like this before," Thorfinna said. She was speaking almost softly now, like she too had caught the vibe of the place. "I know centuries ago, meeting here was originally because of these stones. But for as long as I've been coming here, we've always met under the tree. Whatever these stones represent, I thought it was lost to time."

"Reginleif is older than any of us," Hulda said. Then she glanced over at Njorun. Njorun stood quietly, her face lost in the rippling layers of her hoods, especially as she had her head bowed over the body. If she was even listening to the rest of us, she made no sign. Hulda gave me a little shrug, and I nodded.

Njorun might be older, but no one would ever get an intelligible answer out of her about that.

"Do you know these stones, Njorun?" I asked.

"Stones, stones, stones," she whispered. Sustained screaming had strained her already raspy voice, and the breeze in the grass was almost louder than she was.

"What killed her, do you think?" Kara asked me.

"I don't know. Yet," I said. "My sketchbook is back at the wagon."

"We don't have to worry about touching things before the officials from the modern world do here," Nilda reminded me.

I had no great desire to touch that body, but I had left it long enough for someone else to take charge. Four of us were older, theoretically wiser, and definitely more local than I.

But no one made a move to do anything.

I was going to have to take charge, as unqualified as I felt.

I took a breath. "Right. First thing is, no one leaves this valley. Not until we figure out what happened here. I need everyone's word on that."

To my surprise, it was Njorun who spoke first. "I so swear."

"I so swear," Yngvildr echoed.

"Me, too," Thorfinna said. Then swallowed hard and said, "I so swear."

Nilda and Kara said as one, "I so swear."

"I so swear," I said with an air of closing that matter and moving on to the second thing.

Only the matter wasn't closed yet. Someone hadn't spoken.

I looked at Hulda, and the others blinked, then looked her way too.

She was standing with a sorrowful look on her face, arms crossed as she gazed down at the body. She looked surprised to find us all looking at her.

"What?" she asked innocently. "I already said it."

"No, you didn't," I said.

"Are you sure?" she asked. "Maybe you didn't hear me. Njorun spoke first, then—"

"Just say it," Thorfinna growled at her.

"Swearing twice doesn't hold me to my word any stronger," she said with a glower. But then she threw up her hands and sighed. "Fine. I so swear."

I didn't like the way she had spoken those words. Saying them twice didn't make it twice as binding, I agreed with her there. But saying them with no intention made them meaningless, too. Only I had no idea how I would even call her out on that.

Hulda folded her arms again, looked me straight in the eye, and said, "I so swear."

There was a vibration to the air when she spoke. It reminded me of when my grandmother used her magically enhanced commanding voice to get people to stop arguing and listen to her. Hulda wasn't giving me any kind of command. But there was definitely a touch of magic in her words.

They were binding.

"Thank you," I said. "Now, I need a little space to examine this scene. Nilda and Kara, I'll need your help. The rest of you, can you wait back in the camp? This will only take a moment, and then I'll meet you there and we can discuss what happens next."

"Certainly," Yngvildr said brightly, then gestured for the others to follow her.

"These two are all the help you need?" Hulda asked, lingering where she was even as Yngvildr tugged at her arm.

"They've worked with me before. They understand my methods," I said. Then I felt compelled to add, "and there's also Mjolner."

Hulda looked down at the cat as if only then noticing he was there.

"Of course. Mjolner," she said. Then she turned to follow the others back to camp. Thorfinna was talking about breakfast, but I doubted even she could be hungry.

There wasn't much blood on those stones or on Reginleif's body, but the air was still coppery thick with the smell of it. That, plus the lingering effects of the hangover, had killed any appetite I might have had.

Kara nudged me, a smile in her eyes if not on her lips. "We understand your methods?"

"The funniest thing about that is the idea I have methods," I said. "I just would rather not have strangers hovering."

"May I touch her?" Nilda asked.

"Go ahead," I said, grateful not to do it myself.

Nilda knelt down carefully on the grass, avoiding where the blood pooled.

"No spatter," I noted.

"And no wound that I can see," Nilda said as she gently turned the body over. "There's blood on her dress, but it looks like it dripped there from her hand or something else. There are no cuts."

"She cut her hand to color the stones," Kara said, then looked up at me, and I realized that had been a question.

"I don't know much about these kinds of things," I admitted.

"It's old magic, if magic was what she was doing," Kara said.

"Look," Nilda said. She had been wiping the blood from Reginleif's hand with the hem of Reginleif's skirt. The congealed mass had wiped away, leaving the whorls of her skin stained pink and red and brown.

But in the center of her palm was a puckered scar.

"That's the wound?" Kara said. Then she looked at what was on the grass and stones. "It's a deep gash. Especially if she cut it more than once, that could account for what we see."

"But not for her being dead," I said.

"No, that must've been something else," Kara said.

"Now I *do* wish we were in the modern world," I sighed. "We could really use a medical examiner and an autopsy about now."

"Maybe it was poison," Nilda said, looking closely at Reginleif's face. Then she peeled back her eyelids. "Bloodshot. Do you see?"

Bloodshot didn't seem like the right word to me. Working at a 24-hour diner in St. Paul, I had seen all manner of bloodshot eyes in my customers, whether from long work shifts or from alcohol or less legal substances. But what was going on with the whites of her eyes was more than that.

"Freyja's eyes looked like that. Don't you remember?" Kara said to her sister. "She was in labor for four days delivering baby Martin. Hard labor. That's what that looks like."

"I suppose another great, sustained exertion could have a similar effect," I said. "But what?"

"If only we knew what she was doing," Nilda said.

"We know it was magic," I said. "This place is humming with it."

"I felt something yesterday too," Nilda said. "When I came here alone. There was no blood on the stones then. And the grass wasn't so trampled as now. But I could feel the power of the place. It filled my chest."

"Do you feel more now?" I asked.

Nilda closed her eyes. She stayed still for a long moment, and I listened to the breeze through the grass, and the more distant call of birds fishing the pools under the waterfalls. The sun was warm again, pleasant on my skin.

It was going to be a gorgeous spring day. Despite everything.

Nilda opened her eyes with a little shake of her head. "I don't know. I think it feels different, but maybe I'm thinking about it too hard."

"I wish I'd come out here yesterday, but without knowing what was going to happen here, who knows how much I would've paid attention?" I said.

"It feels disordered to me," Kara said, her eyes half-closed. "Like a pond still rippling from a pebble thrown into it."

"But you might be thinking about it too hard, too," Nilda said.

"No, I think she's right," I said. "Reginleif came here because it was a place of power, then. And she wanted to do some ritual, but alone, away from the others. Was she trying to draw some of that power into herself? Or to replenish its power from herself?"

"It looks like the latter, doesn't it?" Nilda said.

"Maybe it was some kind of exchange," Kara said.

"Maybe," I agreed. "But I think it's clear that something interrupted her before she was finished. That's why things feel unsettled."

"Something killed her to stop the ritual? Or stopped the ritual because they knew it would kill her?" Kara mused.

"If we knew, we'd be a lot closer to figuring out who did this," I said.

Then I sighed. The time had come for the real question of the morning. "This could take time to figure out. Maybe days. We all know we're on a mission of great urgency, as slowly as it's been going for us."

"We needed to find her to get her help, and now she's gone," Nilda said.

I nodded, not trusting myself to speak. My real fear was that she was dead because she had been helping us. But maybe that was my paranoia talking. I was still feeling a lot like a jinx who left a trail of murders everywhere she went. Even here, far from anywhere, where only a small number of people gathered, and only once a year.

Until I turned up.

"We have to stay and solve this," Kara said. "I mean, even if we wanted to go on, where would we go? These women were supposed to have advice for us, and I have yet to hear any useful thing from any of them."

"I didn't press," I admitted. "It felt like there'd be more time for that today, after the festivities were over."

"So we press tomorrow or the next day, when the festivities and the investigation are over," Nilda said, getting to her feet. "If you're asking us to vote, Ingrid, I vote to stay and solve this."

"That's what the Thors would want us to do," Kara said surely.

Mjolner meowed as if casting his own vote. I supposed if he had voted to go, he'd be gone already. But he was sitting beside Reginleif, pawing gently at her uninjured hand.

"So that's four votes to stay and resolve this," I said. "Come on. Let's go tell the others. See what they have to say about it all."

"I almost wish Njorun would speak," Kara said to me as we headed back towards the camp. "I feel like she knows more than she says."

I didn't answer. My own feeling was a little more complicated. To me, it was like Njorun knew things, wanted to tell them, but couldn't get them out. Like her aged body was failing her so badly, she could barely get words out of it anymore.

There had been such frustration in that scream. Frustration and grief.

I just hoped she could find another way to help us.

CHAPTER EIGHT

THE OTHERS HAD GATHERED around the still smoldering remains of the bonfire from the night before. As much as Thorfinna had been talking about breakfast, none of them looked like they'd made any moves in that direction. They just sat quietly on the stools we had been drinking on the night before, looking morosely into the embers.

"Reginleif was murdered," I told them all as Nilda, Kara and I approached. None of them looked shocked or surprised.

"Stabbed?" Thorfinna asked with a dubious frown.

"No," I said, before she could point out the lack of blood. "She had cut her own hand. That's where the blood came from. Part of a ritual."

"How did she die?" Yngvildr asked.

"I was hoping maybe you could help me with that," I admitted. "If she was poisoned, would you be able to tell?"

"It depends on the poison," Yngvildr said.

"If she was poisoned, we were all poisoned," Thorfinna said. "We drank from the same horns and shared the same food. We should all be dead."

"Unless it was on the blade of her knife," Nilda said.

"I should look at that blade," Yngvildr said, standing up.

My heart sank. We had never seen a knife. It hadn't been in Reginleif's other hand, or laying on the grass around her. It hadn't been under her body when we moved it, or sheathed at her belt.

"We haven't found that yet," I admitted. "I'm not done examining the crime scene."

Which was true. I hadn't even started, really. I was too used to drawing things first, then examining them more closely after the drawing gave me leads.

Hey, what do you know? I *did* have methods.

"Yngvildr should examine the body. Maybe Hulda too, if she thinks there is something she would notice that the rest of us would not," Thorfinna said.

"Whatever would I notice?" Hulda asked, surprised. "My magic is a small, rudimentary thing. I wouldn't even know how to start going about killing someone with it, let alone detecting how it was done on someone else by some actually powerful magic-user."

Thorfinna made a grunting noise that was surprisingly articulate at conveying her skepticism of this self-assessment. I rather agreed with her.

But Hulda just made a dismissive wave in my general direction and said, "if this one can't sort it out, she should summon her grandmother."

"I'm not doing that," I said.

"Why not, dear?" Yngvildr asked.

I opened and shut my mouth a few times before I found the words. "She is needed where she is," I said in the end.

There was no way I was going to announce to anyone in the north that my grandmother was recovering from overtaxing her own magic. Or say anything that implied my magic was—what had been Hulda's words?—a small, rudimentary thing. Even if it was.

No one had to know how exposed Villmark was. Not even our allies. Certainly not our foes.

And I wasn't sure I could tell one from the other. Or who was friendly to us, but too free a talker with other, less friendly folk.

"Very well," Thorfinna said, steering the conversation back to her previous point. "Yngvildr should look over the body, but once she is satisfied, we should observe the funerary rites Reginleif would have wanted. Once her bones have been put to rest, we can deal with the rest of this."

"Looking to hide something, Thorfinna?" Hulda asked mildly.

"I offered for you to examine the body yourself," Thorfinna growled at her.

Hulda laughed. "No need. If you had killed her, we would all be able to tell. I'm sure her head would be cleaved from her body. And your sword would still be buried in the corpse."

"You're not wrong," Thorfinna said, still bear-like in her demeanor. "If I had call to kill someone, there'd be no skulking around after. I would show all the world what I had done, and all would know why. And that it was just."

"Why do you want to bury the body first?" Kara asked mildly.

"It's what Reginleif would have wanted," Thorfinna said, less growly now.

"That is correct," Yngvildr said reluctantly. "She was very worried about what would happen to her when she died. I suppose we all are, living out in the wilds on our own as we do."

"No, it was more for Reginleif," Hulda said. "She was something more than us. I don't know what I mean, so don't ask, but it was like she glowed with a power like no other. She was no volva or witch or anything like that, but she was something. And she didn't want her body to decay where anyone could trifle with it."

"Bones, bones, bones," Njorun rattled.

Somehow, that was the most compelling argument of all. Just something in her voice or her posture told me. It really did have to happen right away.

"What has to be done?" I asked.

"I'll wash and wrap the body," Yngvildr said. "I can examine it for signs of poisoning at the same time. Nilda, will you assist me?"

"Certainly," Nilda said.

"I'll need permission to leave the valley," Thorfinna said. "I'll leave my wagon here, so you'll know I'll return. I'll take my horse and Yngvildr's cart back to the forest for more wood for the fire."

"I'll go with her," Kara volunteered.

"Fine with me," Thorfinna said.

Which left me alone at the fire with Njorun and Hulda. I'm not sure which creeped me out more.

"I'll gather flowers," Hulda said suddenly. "I'll stay where you can see me."

"Thank you," I said, although the sarcasm in her words hadn't been lost on me.

I started to head back to where I had left my backpack leaning against the wheel of Reginleif's wagon, but something caught my wrist in an iron grip and wouldn't let me go.

It was Njorun.

She was looking at my hand, my left hand. She turned it over and flattened it out, running her sandpaper-dry skin over my palm again and again. She touched this place and that. At first I thought she was trying to tell my future.

But then I had the sense that what she was really doing was examining my palm for signs of healed wounds. Like if I had cut my palm sometime in the past like Reginleif had done at the stones.

"Do you know what the stones are?" I asked her.

She looked up at me, pinning me with those milky blue eyes. "Old," she told me, gripping my hand more tightly in both of hers. "Danger-ous." Then she looked down at her own fingers digging deeply into my flesh and released me all at once. She held her hands up before her own eyes as if the sight of them shocked her. She touched her cheek and gave a startled cry at the feel of it sagging from her skull.

"Njorun?" I said.

She looked up at me again, but less intensely than before. I was losing her again. But then she said, "wondrous," and walked away.

Was she still talking about those stones? I had no clue.

Thorfinna and Kara returned with a cartful of wood. Most of it was for the bonfire itself, but Thorfinna had also cut a few pieces, which she used now to craft a very basic sort of bier.

She had just finished when Nilda and Yngvildr emerged from the grass with a wrapped bundle between them. It looked too small to be

Reginleif, but of course it was. Thorfinna helped them lift it onto the bier. Then she stacked the wood under it.

Hulda stepped up next, strewing what looked like every spring flower in the entire meadow over the top of the bier. When her arms were empty, she pressed her hand on the end of the bundle where Reginleif's head must be. She bent down and whispered something to the corpse. Then she turned away.

But as she walked, the hand that brushed against her side darted behind her. Her fingers made a soundless snapping motion, and the bonfire suddenly caught light.

A voice filled the meadow, singing a song I didn't know in a language that was almost familiar. It had to be some older version of Norse, older than what we spoke in Villmark, older even than the words all the women here had been speaking before we came among them.

The song brought tears to my eyes, and I wasn't the only one. It echoed under the bows of that tree. It was like the waterfalls quieted their own cascades to let that song carry louder.

It was only as the song was ending that I realized it had been Njorun who had been singing. And the very instant she stopped, she turned away from the flames and walked away from the rest of us to stand alone nearer to the stones.

For the second time in as many days, time lost all meaning. We stood around that fire, watching as it consumed the flowers, the bier, the wrappings, and Reginleif herself.

I woke again at dawn. I had fallen asleep sitting up with my back against the stool behind me. Mjolner was in my arms, not sleeping. He was watching the remains of the fire smoking still, his yellow-green eyes as inscrutable as ever.

Then I saw Yngvildr was awake too. Without a word, she got up, then started poking through the remains of the fire. She had a basket with her, filled with a few of the flowers from the day before she had rescued from the flames. She pushed aside the embers with a hard-ened stick, retrieving bone after bone until she had placed them all into that basket.

The others were awake now too, and we left the wagons, horse and ox behind, Thorfinna in the lead with that basket in her arms, walking back towards the edge of the woods.

We didn't go into that wood, although it felt like it was watching us as we dug a hole, put the bones in, then covered it all up again.

Thorfinna had carved a stave to serve as a marker, and she pounded it deep into the ground. For a moment I was startled to see the reidh rune there. But of course it belonged there. It was the first letter in Reginleif's name.

Yngvildr put the last of the flowers around the marker, and we all stood silently together for a moment.

Then, without a word between us, we walked back to the camp. We gathered again around the remains of the bonfire, but none of us sat down.

"Her wagon is yours now, I believe?" Thorfinna said. She had spoken softly for her, but after so long without a sound, it made me jump.

"Why would it be mine?" I asked.

"Because you need it," Yngvildr said with a kind smile.

I wasn't sure how having an ox and wagon was going to help me find the Thors. From the little traveling I had done with it, it had been slower than walking, and that had been still on a road. Where we were going, there would likely be few roads. The wagon would be a liability for us.

Then Hulda let out an exasperated sigh. "If it bothers you that much, you can use my tent. It's the roomiest. I just assumed it was tainted in your eyes or something."

"Tainted?" I said, feeling more lost than ever.

"I've had your grandmother's man in it more times than I can count," she said, and I immediately wished I could retroactively shove my fingers in my ears.

"You need to question us, right?" Thorfinna said, after scowling darkly at Hulda.

"The wagon is more private," Kara said. Clearly, she had caught on faster than me.

But even after understanding all that, I hesitated. I really wanted to draw the scene first. I knew from the past that it didn't matter how much time passed. What I drew never seemed to depend on freshness or anything like that.

I just wasn't prepared to face these women one by one. They were... a lot.

"Everyone stays until it's solved," Nilda said sternly. "No one gets dismissed just because Ingrid has run out of questions for the time being. Understood?"

Her hand was on the hilt of her sword again. Thorfinna raised an amused eyebrow at that, but just grinned.

"We all understand," Hulda said. "But it would be easier to be understanding if things were moving along. Am I wrong?"

"She's not wrong," Yngvildr sighed. "Spring is a crucial time of year for me."

"So is fall. And summer," Hulda said. "Winter is probably convenient for you to be delayed."

"Actually, I never leave my cottage in the winter," Yngvildr said, her cheeks going scarlet. "I steep, infuse and mix herbs. The timing and conditions have to be just right when mixing tinctures. I can't do that on the road."

"Well, I have all the time in the world," Thorfinna announced. "But if no one else is going to step up, I'd gladly go first."

"All right," I said gratefully. If they'd asked me to pick who I wanted to talk to first, I would've chosen Thorfinna.

Although as I opened the wagon door, I had second thoughts. The space inside was tight, and Thorfinna was going to take up most of it.

Hopefully, this wouldn't take long.

CHAPTER NINE

I HAD ONLY BEEN inside the wagon once before, when I had put the lunch things away the day we had all met on the road. Now I found that Mjolner was once more all curled up sleeping on the bed as if it were his and he had slept there a thousand times before.

But it seemed like Thorfinna had never been inside this space. She had to turn sideways to get her shoulders through the doorframe for one thing. Then she hovered there, half-bent over because of the lowness of the roof, and just took the whole scene in. Every item on every shelf, as if making a mental inventory.

But she didn't try to touch anything. She just settled herself oh so gently on one of the stools at the table. I squeezed in across from her and folded my hands on the tabletop.

"I wanted to start with you, actually," I admitted. "My memories of the night in question are a blur. I have a feeling you remember more."

"More than you, or more than anyone?" Thorfinna asked with laughter in her eyes. "No one has ever yet accused Thorfinna of not holding her mead."

"What do you remember?" I asked, and her face grew serious again.

"You dropped out first," she said. "I was up the longest. Well, except for Njorun. I don't think that woman actually sleeps."

I blinked, and realized that was likely true. I had never seen her eat or drink. I had never seen her sleep.

Then I quickly added a few more things to that list. She had no pack that I had seen, not so much as a blanket to wrap herself in or a stick to walk with. She was just there, always, hovering like a ghost with no more possessions in the world than the tattered remains of her clothing.

Weird.

"You slept in your wagon?" I guessed, forcing my mind back on the task at hand.

"No. Usually do, but not at the Dísablót," she said. "I like to sleep under the stars, close to the fire. I don't know when exactly it was that I fell asleep. I want to say it was pretty close to dawn, but the sky to the east wasn't any lighter yet, so maybe not. And I woke up when Njorun started screaming, same as the rest of us."

"Do you know where anyone else was while you were awake?" I asked.

"I could see everyone, actually," she said. "You were sleeping by the wagon. Your friends were close by you when they collapsed. Hulda went into her tent, but she had the flaps open to let in the breeze. It was a warm night, remember? I could see her in there. And Yngvildr was in her tent, too. She was the first one to go to bed after you. Her flaps were closed, but they faced the fire. I never saw her go out. Njorun just flitted about, like she does. I think that's everyone accounted for?"

I nodded. Well, I had the bare bones of the time frame worked out, at least.

"How well did you know Reginleif?" I asked.

"We've met time and again on the road and here at the Dísablót," Thorfinna said. "I wouldn't say I knew her well, but she would stop to talk with me from time to time."

"What about? The weather, or travel conditions, or the like?" I asked.

"Ha! Not Reginleif," Thorfinna laughed. "No, that woman loved her solitude too much to sacrifice it for chitchat. If she stopped to talk, there was something she needed to know or something that she needed to have done."

"Like what?" I asked.

"Well, to tell the truth, she mostly asked me about your boys. The Thors," Thorfinna said. "I thought it was odd when she sent you three to ask me about them. I would swear she watches them far more closely than I do."

"She does?" I asked. "But she told us when we met her that she didn't know them."

"Is that what she said?" Thorfinna asked me. I was about to insist it was, but something in the way she was looking at me made me scan my memories again.

"She said she knew nothing that would help us on our quest," I said. "But if she knew where the Thors were, why didn't she just say so?"

"Isn't it obvious?" Thorfinna asked. I shook my head. "Telling you that wouldn't have helped you on your quest. Just like she told you."

"That doesn't make any sense," I said.

"Sure it does," she insisted. "Look, what if they were on the moon? And she knew that's where they were. Even if she told you, it wouldn't help you. How are the three of you going to get to the moon? So what's the point in telling you?" She ended with a shrug.

"They aren't on the moon," I said. "And anyway, she told us we had to go to the Dísablót to talk to all of you. That one of you would help us."

"That's probably true, then," Thorfinna said with a satisfied nod.

"Only none of you have helped us," I said.

"Not yet, maybe," she said with another shrug. "We're all still here. Who knows what will be revealed?"

"Do you know where they are?" I asked, rubbing at the growing headache in my temples.

"Everything I told you was the truth, and I told you everything," Thorfinna said. "I was thinking more about the others. Clearly, someone here is keeping secrets. Someone here killed Reginleif, somehow."

"What if I asked you to guess who did that?" I asked.

"Well, Yngvildr knows a lot about plants. Medicines and poisons both. She knows ways to kill people without leaving a sign. And if she was the only one here who knew anything about that sort of thing, she wouldn't even have to be very careful about it."

"You think Yngvildr is a murderer?" I asked.

"I didn't say that. I'm just saying she could. I don't know any reason she'd have to kill Reginleif. But if she had one, she could do it," Thorfinna said.

I had to agree that was likely true. I briefly entertained the desire to learn more about plants and poisons, since they kept coming up in these investigations.

Then I remembered all of Haraldr's books I hadn't read yet, just about runes and volva magic. Plants and poisons would have to wait.

It was a good thing my family was long-lived.

"What about Njorun?" I asked. "She was still awake when you fell asleep, you mentioned. And she wasn't there when you woke up."

"Neither were you," Thorfinna pointed out. "I suppose it's possible. I don't really understand Njorun."

"When she talks?" I asked.

"Anything about her. She's a strange one," Thorfinna said. "I'd say she was not entirely human, but I think that was true of Reginleif, too. Being in the north changes a person. Not me. I'm still me. But other people, sometimes."

"What about Hulda?" I asked.

I expected her to be dismissive of Hulda and her small, rudimentary magic, but I wasn't exactly surprised when she instead shuddered at the mere mention of her name.

"Don't like her," she whispered. "I can't say why. That little spark that started the bonfire was the biggest thing I've ever seen her do, and it wasn't exactly impressive. I had a brand from the other fire in my hand already. I was about to start it on my own."

"There is a woman in Villmark by the name of Halldis," I said, and realized I was whispering too.

"Don't know her," Thorfinna said.

"Hulda reminds me of her," I said. "A lot."

"In what way?" Thorfinna asked.

"Like Halldis, Hulda uses a lot of magic to alter her appearance," I said. "One minute, she's young and beautiful. The next she's older. And I guess still beautiful," I was forced to admit.

"Oh, that?" Thorfinna said with a dismissive wave. "That's so common."

"Where?" I asked.

Thorfinna pressed her lips together in thought. "All right, I'll amend that. It used to be common. There used to be more villages in the wilds. Villmarkers used to range out further, and there were other communities that had nothing to do with Villmark. I've seen everything from Old Norway to here, and while it's always been more wild than civilization, trust me when I tell you there used to be more people."

"I believe you," I assured her. "I've seen the ruins of villages. But they're old."

"Yeah, sorry," Thorfinna said with a flinch. "You have to remember time is hard for us to measure out here, okay? But lots of those villages, when there used to be villages, had resident women in them who had a sort of witchcraft. They weren't volvas. Volvas, you pretty much only encounter around kings."

"Or councils," I said, thinking of Villmark.

"Exactly! You get me," Thorfinna said. "These other women had smaller power. They usually peddled in love spells and curses. The kind of things that mostly never worked. But making themselves look young and comely? That was their chief power. And, hey! I'm not knocking it. Most of them got pretty far with just that."

"What happened to all the villages?" I asked.

Thorfinna's merry glow tamped down to a grave seriousness once more. "That's not something I can give a simple answer to at all. It wasn't just one thing everywhere, like famine or invaders or something. It was just… I guess it was just time? In the end, that's what's going to take all of us."

"That's not what got Reginleif, though," I said.

"Isn't it?" she mused. "She wasn't a volva or witch, but she had some sort of power that wasn't quite human. And she was clearly doing something with that power, out there with those stones. I don't understand a bit of it, I'm afraid. But I can still feel it in my bones. Something took Reginleif before her time. And I don't think we sent it all back into the universe when we dealt with her body. I think some of it was already gone."

"Like it was taken from her?" I asked.

"I don't think there's a power in the world that could take something from her without her consent. Not even by force," Thorfinna said. Then barked out a humorless chuckle. "I keep talking about her like she's still here, don't I?"

"It's okay. I think we're all doing that," I said.

"Yeah," she said, sad again. "But no. If I'm right and Reginleif was short a bit of her power when she died, it wasn't taken by force. But it was definitely stolen. And I have no idea who would be clever enough to pull that off. Don't really want to think about it." She shuddered, then attempted to plaster her usual smile back on her face. "That's really all I know, and more than I should've just speculated about. Can I go?"

"Yes, thank you," I said.

It took a bit of work for her to get back out of that narrow doorway. It gave me a moment or two to mull over what she had said.

I really needed to draw that crime scene, but perhaps this was the better way to do it. To have more information first. Three more interviews, and I would be ready to draw.

But I couldn't shake the growing feeling that all of this was, in some way I couldn't grasp, connected to the Thors.

It bothered me that Reginleif had been so sneaky in her answer to me when we met. She hadn't seemed untrustworthy, ever. So why hide the truth? Why give me a half-answer, a misdirection?

Because she wanted us all to be there at the Dísablót?

Had she intended to help us for real on the next step in our journey once we were done here? It was a possibility.

But had the ritual that killed her been an interruption, or the entire point of being here?

There didn't seem to be any way to get those answers now. Maybe there never would be. But in the meantime, I smiled politely and bid Yngvildr come in to the wagon that I was already treating like my own place.

CHAPTER TEN

YNGVILDR LOOKED around the wagon interior with great interest. She even sniffed the air, which had me doing the same. I could smell something like dried herbs, but only faintly, and it wasn't anything I could identify. Perhaps Yngvildr could. I wondered what it told her.

She adjusted the stool across from mine, then sat down, smoothing her long skirt over her lap, then looking at me attentively.

"Have you been in here before?" I asked.

"I don't think any of us have," she said. "Reginleif was a very private person."

"She sent me inside to put some dishes away less than an hour after she met me," I said.

"Really?" Yngvildr said with open surprise. But then she nodded her head to the pendant around my neck. "That probably had something to do with it. Do you know the history between her and your grandmother?"

"Only that they met here, in the north, and that they were friends and, I guess, travel companions," I said. "I gather their friendship ended when my grandmother settled down in Villmark and Runde and stopped traveling so far from home."

"They were very close," Yngvildr said. "I'm older than I look, you know."

"Isn't everyone?" I asked.

"Some more than others," she said. "For instance, Reginleif to me always looked the same. No older, no younger. But I can remember when your grandmother looked your age."

"Really?" I said, suddenly keenly interested. "What was she like?"

"Wild," Yngvildr said with a laugh.

"What, like a party girl?" I asked. That was a stretch with my still basic Villmark Norse, but she laughed in understanding.

"No, no. I meant, she was very much of this place. This valley is pretty tame, but further into the mountains, things get very different. And that was where I would have sworn she felt the most at home," Yngvildr said. "I mostly saw her here, at the Dísablóts, but she always came with such stories. Things she and Reginleif had seen together. Adventures they had had. All in this wagon."

She looked around again, and I was once more sure she was perceiving more than I. But maybe it wasn't anything I should be seeing. Maybe it was more like everything around us triggered another memory for her.

"I only intend to use this wagon for this investigation. It doesn't feel like it's supposed to be mine," I said.

"No, I think you should take it with you, back to Villmark," Yngvildr said, reaching across the table to squeeze my hand in emphasis. "Nora should have it."

That felt right. The minute she said it, I knew that was what I had to do. I should've thought of it before, really.

"You want to ask me about the night of the Dísablót," she said, drawing my mind back to the present.

"I do," I said. "My own memory is hazy."

"I'm not surprised," she said, and sounded annoyed.

"Did I do something embarrassing?" I asked.

"Oh, no! I'm just irritated with Thorfinna. You kept trying to turn her down when she pressed that horn on you, but that woman just won't take no for an answer. Well, and there's the proof, isn't it?" she said.

It took me a minute to realize what she was referring to. She had to push back my sleeve for me to notice it. Purple bruises, like someone had gripped my forearm too tightly. To keep me from leaving the party?

"I don't remember this at all," I said, rolling back the sleeve of my flannel shirt to look at the fading marks more closely. "It doesn't feel like anything now. And I do bruise really easily."

"She bullied you. Don't defend her," Yngvildr said. "You got away from her in the end, but that only had her turning on your friends. I'm surprised they were able to get up in the morning at all."

I made a mental note to ask Nilda and Kara about that, but I had a sinking feeling that their memories of the night were even more fragmented than mine.

And Yngvildr was clearly trying to imply that had been deliberate on Thorfinna's part.

"How much of the celebration did you really see?" I asked her. "I understand you turned in shortly after I did."

"I did," she admitted. "I'm not a night person. At all. I only stayed up as late as I did in case you ended up needing an advocate."

"But you didn't do the same with my friends?" I asked.

"They seemed to be better able to stand up to Thorfinna," she said. "Or maybe I told myself that because I just couldn't stay awake any longer. I collapsed into my bedroll the minute I was inside my tent, and I was off to dreamland the minute my head hit the pillow."

"And when you woke up?" I asked.

"I woke up when Njorun was screaming," she said. "I came out of my tent to see the others sitting up from wherever they had fallen asleep the night before. I don't think any of us were up already save you and Njorun. But I suppose someone might have been pretending to wake up just then."

"What do you know about the stones?" I asked her.

"I've seen Reginleif there before, when we all gather here for the

Dísablót. But she never took anyone with her when she went to do…whatever it was she was doing. Not even your grandmother, back when they were close and traveling together. It was her private thing," Yngvildr said. Then she shifted her position on her stool, leaning closer to ask me, "what do you notice about this wagon? What's here and what's missing?"

I looked around, trying to see it with new eyes. But all I saw was what I had seen the first time I had stepped inside it with a stack of clean dishes in my arms.

"It's a cozy little rolling home," I said. "I can sort of feel how much she loved this space. But nothing else."

"So what's missing?" Yngvildr asked me with the air of a teacher who was absolutely not going to let me off the hook just because I had failed to do the homework.

I thought about it. Then I looked over my shoulder at the sleeping form of Mjolner. But he was no help.

Then I had it. "There's nothing magical here," I said. "But is that odd? Reginleif wasn't a volva or any other sort of witch, was she? You all keep telling me that."

"She was some sort of something," Yngvildr said vaguely. "She had power. We all saw it last night when we were dancing. Or did you forget that?"

"No," I said. That memory was clear. Reginleif dancing, like a being of bright golden light.

"Reginleif was older than any of us," Yngvildr said. "I suppose if we could ever figure it all out, we'd put Thorfinna's birth in Old Norway earlier than Reginleif's birth in your hometown of Villmark. But Reginleif came to the wilds of the north as a small child and stayed longer in the deeper places than any of us. Thorfinna was nearly grown before she got lost in the mountains and ended up here. And whatever she brags about, Thorfinna skirts the edges of the deeper places, just like the rest of us do."

"That's what gave Reginleif power? Her travels?" I pondered.

"Maybe?" Yngvildr said. "I tried to ask her, more than once, but she was never open about any of that. Whatever plants grow in those places, she wouldn't tell me a thing about them. And how she got in and out of those places intact, she would never tell me either."

"Do you think that's what she used her power for? Staying safe while she traveled?" I asked.

"I'm not sure she ever *used* her power for anything," Yngvildr said. "I think it was just a part of her. Like her blood. Some people shake off diseases better than others, even without the help of medicines, right? I think Reginleif was just naturally better able to handle the wilds. But then again, she also felt more at home there."

"If she took my grandmother with her to those places, was that because my grandmother was also immune, or was Reginleif capable of protecting her somehow?" I asked.

Yngvildr's face lit up. "Ooh, interesting question! That is one to ponder."

"I suppose I can ask my grandmother when I get back home," I said. If she had an immunity, I might have it too. That sort of thing could come in handy.

On the other hand, if Reginleif had done something to protect her, that would mean she *did* do some sort of active magic. Although Yngvildr was right, nothing inside her home gave any hint of that. No magic herbs or bronze wands. No books of lore or rune staves. Nothing.

"So Reginleif showed no signs of poisoning when you cleaned her body," I said.

"No, none," Yngvildr said. Then she scoffed. "Although I suppose Thorfinna told you that *of course* I'd say that. It's just what a guilty person would say, too."

"Is she wrong?" I asked as diplomatically as I could.

"I doubt very much I could hide anything from you," she said. "When we were all still feasting together, before the drinking started, I was chatting with your friend Nilda about you. She told me all about the other crimes you've solved. She didn't go into a lot of details on how you do it, but it was pretty clear that through magic you always find the guilty party in the end."

"So far," I said.

"Well, if I was planning a murder, and I heard that, would I have carried on with my plans, anyway?" Yngvildr said. "Either I would wait until you were gone and try to catch Reginleif out on the road somewhere, alone and unprotected, or I would remove you from the situation myself first. Right?"

"You've given this some thought," I said.

"Were you paying any attention when we were all eating?" she asked.

"To what?" I asked.

"To what we ate," she said.

"You mean what *you* ate," I said, remembering. Actually, now that I was thinking about it, it was weird that Thorfinna hadn't brought it up. It was the one way Yngvildr could've poisoned everyone but herself, if that had been her plan. "You didn't eat any of the meat."

"Very good," Yngvildr said, apparently back in teacher mode. "I never eat meat. Not since I left my village decades ago. When I'm out on my own, I just can't bear to kill a living thing. I gave up on snaring rabbits almost at once. I tried to push myself to keep catching and eating fish, but in the end I just couldn't do it. It was the eyes, I think. They were always so sad, looking up at me."

"I'm not sure I see the connection," I admitted.

"I can't kill things," she said. "I couldn't have killed Reginleif. I don't have it in me."

"Well, poisoning is a very different thing than butchering," I said.

"But she wasn't poisoned, I promise you," Yngvildr said. "I mean, what happened to her, it was obviously magic, wasn't it?"

"I'm not so sure," I said. "I usually feel that. Even when I don't want to. All I felt in that place was a disruption of the old power in the stones, I think. Nothing of active malice. Believe me, I've felt that before. It's unmistakable."

"I hope you don't think I'm accusing *you*," she said earnestly.

I belatedly realized it might have sounded that way. But I knew I wasn't guilty, so I hadn't caught it. But to any of the others, I was the one who had found Reginleif. I could've killed her, then waited to tell the others. Or was still working on getting rid of the body when Njorun found me.

"I know I'm not a suspect, but I can see where that wouldn't carry weight with the rest of you," I said.

"No, I don't think any of us think you did this," she said firmly. "You and your friends are here to find the Thors. Reginleif was helping you with that. Why would you turn on her? It makes no sense."

Maybe because she wasn't actually helping us?

Not that I was going to say that thought out loud.

"So you think it was Hulda?" I asked.

"Hulda? Oh my, no," Yngvildr said. "That little trick with the fire? That's more magic than I've ever seen her do."

"She made it look pretty casual," I said.

"I think she was showing off for you," Yngvildr said. "You threaten her. Just like Nora did, long ago. Do you have a lover?"

That question certainly came out of nowhere. I just gaped at her, unable to summon an answer.

She laughed at the look on my face, then waved her hand as if to dispel the effects of her question. "I'm just saying, she went after that man Frór only because of who she thought he was to Nora. And how spitting mad was she when Nora didn't even care? But if you do have someone special, better not let her know. She'll be after him in a heartbeat. Or her," she added with a shrug.

"I'll keep that in mind," I said, my mouth suddenly dry. If Hulda wanted to target a man to get to me and wasn't too concerned about making sure she'd picked the right mark, there were all sorts of people who could be in danger.

I didn't have someone special, not one person. I didn't have the time, with my studies and with all the investigations that kept cropping up.

But I had a lot of close friends. And an outsider could get the wrong idea about a lot of them pretty easily.

"So that's the kind of trouble you have to watch out for with Hulda," Yngvildr went on. "But magical murder? Not so much."

"So who then?" I asked.

She shuddered, then leaned in to whisper, "Njorun. You must sense it."

"But why?" I asked.

"I never understand a word that woman says. How am I supposed to understand the workings of her mind?" Yngvildr said. "I just know my skin creeps whenever she's near."

I had to admit mine did the same. But there was a world of difference between something that was making my hair stand on end out of sheer otherworldly strangeness, and something actively malicious.

And as strange as Njorun was, I didn't feel malice coming from her.

That, and the grief in her cries, the mourning in the song she had sung during the funeral rites. They all felt too real to me.

Whoever had done this, I was pretty sure it wasn't Njorun.

But if magic was the cause, that left only Hulda.

"Thank you for your time, Yngvildr," I said. "Can you send Hulda in when you go?"

It was time to bite the bullet. As Yngvildr stepped down from the wagon, I closed my eyes and tried to clear my mind.

Hulda reminded me of Halldis. Maybe my gut was telling me something, but maybe it was paranoia. The last thing I wanted to do was accuse someone falsely, because of my own prejudices.

I must have been giving off some kind of nervous vibes, because I opened my eyes to find a sleepy Mjolner climbing down from the bunk to curl back up in my lap. I put my hand on his furry head and he purred. I could feel it vibrating against my palm.

I was calm. I was clear. And I was ready.

I looked up as Hulda came into the wagon.

CHAPTER ELEVEN

By now, I was used to the way everyone examined the entire interior of the wagon before turning their attention to me. So I just waited as Hulda looked all around her before sitting on the very edge of the low stool across from me. But there was no curiosity or interest on her face, just a nose-wrinkling disdain. And once she was sitting down, she started to put her folded hands on the table, then thought better of it, setting them instead on her own lap.

There was nothing on that tabletop to offend, but I let that little moment go without comment.

"I suppose you're wondering where I was the night of the Dísablót?" she said. But she didn't wait for me to respond, just went on, "I was up later than you, but then most of us were. When I left the bonfire, only Thorfinna was still particularly alert, and she was still trying to get a little more mead into your two little friends. That woman. She can drink like a bear, but she can never find a companion to match her. Perhaps she should try finding a man."

"And Njorun?" I asked.

"Oh," she said. "I had quite forgotten her. But of course she was there, the whole night. Just lingering around, not really a part of things. You know, like she is."

"Then you went to bed. In your tent, right?" I asked.

"No, actually," she said. "I was doing a bit of magic of my own."

"After drinking and dancing around the bonfire?" I asked.

"I didn't drink so much as you, and my dancing was a bit more intentional," she said. I felt like that last bit was a dig somehow, but it felt like a misdirect.

"What was the magic you were doing?" I pressed.

"Nothing you'd be interested in, dear," she said, but leaned back on the stool, her hands clasping her knee as she rocked. "Just a bit of old magic. I had set out a basin to collect the dew, and once the moonlight had shone on it, I bathed my face with it. It keeps you youthful." She touched her fingers to her cheeks and grinned at me, but as far as I could tell, she looked the same as before.

Her grin faded at my lack of response and she huffed, "I do it every year at the Dísablót, religiously. I never let age creep up on me. It might not seem like any great transformation to you, but I assure you I look very good for my age. Very good."

"That seems to be common with everyone in this area," I said.

She scowled at me. Then a mischievous gleam lit up her eyes. "Some of us are more successful than others, dear. I can provide references, should you need them."

"Why would I need your references?" I asked, and instantly regretted it. This was clearly just another way for her to bring Frór back into the conversation. I held up a hand to belay her response. "Forget it. Never mind."

"Of course, dear," she said, as if she knew full well what I had been thinking. Then her face took on a sorrowful mien. "I don't envy you, this job. It's going to be very tricky indeed, finding the real culprit."

"Why is that?" I asked.

"Any one of us could've done it, couldn't have we?" she said. "Thorfinna made sure the three of you were out of it, forcing drink after drink down your throats. Yngvildr is a master poisoner, and yet she's the one you tasked with clearing her own name." She gave me a chiding tisk at that. But then went on, "and don't even get me started with Njorun. None of us know the first thing about her. Who knows what power she has? Or what her motives are?"

"I think we can rule out Thorfinna," I said. "The only cut on the body was to her palm, and she did that to herself."

"You think so small," Hulda said. "Search her wagon. I'm sure you'll find there a blade as thin as a needle, long and straight, as strong as any sword. A prick like that wouldn't leave a mark that most would notice."

"It also wouldn't kill anyone," I pointed out.

"Not without the correct poison, no," Hulda said.

"Are you saying Yngvildr and Thorfinna were in this together?" I asked.

"I'm saying it's a possibility you have to rule out, dear," she said pityingly.

"They sure do accuse each other a lot for coconspirators," I said.

"The oldest trick in the book, dear," Hulda said.

"Say that's all true. What's their motive?" I asked.

"Ooh, that's the juiciest of all," she said with relish. "But surely you've guessed it already?"

"Enlighten me," I said.

"Well, it's the oldest *motive* in the book," she said.

"Money?" I ventured.

"Men," she said, leaning forward and placing both her palms down on the tabletop to drive home her point. Then she realized what she was doing and sat back, wiping her hands off on the edges of the tablecloth. "Or love. Whatever," she said.

"Thorfinna and Reginleif were after the same man?" I said. I had no problem making that sound deeply skeptical. I couldn't even picture it.

"*Men*," Hulda said again, rolling her eyes. "Your men, in point of fact."

"Wait, you think this is about the Thors?" I asked.

"You seriously haven't considered that already?" she asked me. "It wasn't clear to you from the minute you met them both that they weren't remotely going to help you find them? It was clear to me."

"Are you saying they knew how to find them but lied to us about it?" I asked.

"I'm saying that Reginleif has long considered herself their personal protector. I'm guessing because they are associated with your grandmother," she said with a shrug. "But Thorfinna also considers herself their personal protector. For... other reasons."

"If it's just about protecting them, why wouldn't they just work together?" I asked.

"Reginleif doesn't approve of Thorfinna's methods. I'm certain she told that monstrous woman to stay clear of her boys. And that didn't go over well," Hulda said.

"So you think she wasn't helping the Mikkelsens and me because she doesn't approve of us, either?" I asked. "You don't think she felt she owed something to me because of my grandmother?"

"Oh, dear, I'm sure that's not true," she said. "I'm only saying, I think Reginleif was becoming an obstacle to Thorfinna's desires. But maybe I'm wrong," she ended with a shrug.

I sighed and rubbed at the bridge of my nose. She was maddening to talk to, but in a way the entire conversation was a bit of a relief.

Because if she had really been anything at all like Halldis, she would've tried putting me under some sort of spell already. Whether something to make me believe her, or something to knock me out so she could make her escape, she would've tried something.

And I sensed no power from her. If her spell with the dew and the moonlight had had any effect, even with my magical vision, I saw no sign of it now.

"Yngvildr could've been working alone," Hulda went on, apparently unaware of the way I was looking at her. I blinked back to the real world as she went on. "She could've poisoned us all that night, if she had wanted to."

"It's been pointed out that she didn't partake of any of the meat," I said.

"Oh, Thorfinna mentioned that, did she?" she asked. I half-shrugged, half-nodded. "But I don't think that was the method she chose at all."

"What do you think it was?" I asked.

"That tea," she said.

I had to wrack my brain on that one. It had been right before Thorfinna had brought out the mead. But there *had* been tea. Only I couldn't remember drinking any of it myself.

It would be ironic if Yngvildr had tried to poison us all with tea and been undone by Thorfinna and her bottomless barrel of mead.

If that had even happened.

"I didn't drink any of it myself," Hulda said with a sniff. "For a master of plants, she has a terrible palate. Her teas are all so… grassy."

"I don't think I had any of it myself, so I can't say," I told her. "So you don't suspect Njorun at all?"

"Njorun?" she repeated, as if she was trying to place the name.

"Everyone else seems to be kind of afraid of her," I said.

"Really?" she said. "I wonder why? She's odd, but there's something about her that's just so childlike. You know?"

"Actually, I do," I admitted.

"No, I don't think she's your woman," Hulda said. Then she sighed, "Ingrid Torfudottir, my romantic rivalry with your grandmother aside, I would really love to help you. Both with solving this murder and with your first quest to find your friends. But I'm afraid I'm doomed to come up short with you on both counts."

"Why do you say that?" I asked.

"You don't seem to think much of my theories about the killing, and aside from that, I didn't see anything useful, did I?" she asked.

"I'm not remotely done asking questions, though," I said. "These are just preliminary interviews. I have things I do to get more leads, and then I'll be asking everyone far more pointed things."

"That sounds ominous," Hulda said, her eyes wide. But then she waved it away like I was being silly. "It's possible that you never solve this, you know. And then where will your friends be? I can't imagine delaying here is doing them any good at all."

"That's not really your concern, though, is it?" I said.

"I'm just saying, it sounded urgent when you and your friends first came here. I know you didn't get the answers you were hoping for.

And, like I said, I'm so sorry I'm not able to help more. I know they are in the north, but everyone knows that. I can't be of any better assistance to you."

"It sounds like you're asking me to let you go," I said.

"No, not at all!" she said. "I'm only suggesting, don't wait too long to give up on this."

"Well, like I said, these interviews are only the first step," I said. "I'm far from giving up. And the Thors would understand."

Something in my voice caught her attention, and she was lunging over the table again, looking me very closely in the eye. I wanted to look away, or better yet, put a hand on her face and force her away. But I kept my gaze steady and waited for her to sit back again.

She did, but with a look on her face I really didn't like at all.

"They are the protectors of Villmark, but not the only ones," I said as evenly as I could. "I was sent to bring them home, but home is not undefended without them. Calibrate your sense of our urgency accordingly."

"Of course, my dear," she said, but there was something catlike in her smile as she turned towards the door.

Like I had just provided her with tasty new prey.

Great. Now I had another reason to be sure I found the Thors, sooner rather than later. On the one hand, they were traveling with Frór, who knew who Hulda was. And on the other hand, they weren't fools. They knew well enough to distrust strange yet beautiful women who came on way too strong.

But on the other, other hand…

Yeah, I had to find them first.

Just as soon as I solved this murder.

CHAPTER TWELVE

I DON'T KNOW what I had been expecting to happen when Njorun took her turn climbing into the wagon. A part of me had been afraid she'd start screaming again, and I was half-braced against it, ready to clap my hands over my ears.

But she, like the others, looked around the space first. I couldn't see her face, but the layers of her hood fluttered as she turned her head this way and that.

She ended looking down at me, but her face was still in shadow. I couldn't see her eyes, let alone the expression on her face.

Then Mjolner looked up at her from where he was still sleeping on my lap. He gave her a soft meow that sounded like a polite invitation.

Which I guess it was, as Njorun gave him a quick nod, then settled onto the stool across from me.

"Njorun, thank you for speaking with me," I said.

"Words… come… hard," she stammered. Then she pushed back her hood, and I could see her face clearly. It wasn't any more pleasant in the soft light of the wagon than in the harsh light of day. She smoothed the few wisps of hair she had left over her bare scalp, and once again I got the sense that she was surprised by what she felt, touching her own body.

I wondered what would happen if I showed her her reflection in a mirror. Just imagining it made me shudder. It definitely wasn't the time for that.

"Did you know Reginleif well?" I asked.

Her hands rose up before her, shaping a large round shape, as if she were pantomiming holding a beach ball.

"I'm sorry?" I said.

She sighed. Then she said something, but it was like the language from her funeral song, older Norse than any I knew.

I wished Haraldr were there.

Then she bit her bloodless lip, as if sensing my frustration. Her eyes narrowed in concentration and she managed to utter two words, although in a way that made it sound like they had no relation to each other. "Long. Time."

"Was she a friend? A good friend?" I asked.

Then, suddenly lucid, Njorun said, "I knew your grandmother well. She loved Reginleif, but not like Reginleif loved her. But they together were more than the two of them apart."

"What do you mean?" I asked.

But she was pantomiming the beach ball again. This time it seemed to explode, her hands spreading with fingers wide. But all she said was, "glow."

"I saw Reginleif glow," I said. "It was beautiful."

But Njorun wasn't looking at me anymore. She was gazing fixedly at the corner of the wagon to the left and behind me. Like there was someone there she was arguing with. Her lips were moving, but I didn't hear a word. I turned my head, but there was nothing in that corner save a short broom standing upright in a dry bucket.

"Njorun?" I called, trying to get her attention back. I had to say her name twice more before she looked at me again. But it was like she was making a point to whoever she was arguing with unseen in the corner, using me to performatively ignore them.

"Speedy journey and toil of the steed," she told me with a strange air of triumph. Like she had just made a seminal point.

"Can you tell me where you were all that night?" I asked. "We saw you at the dancing, of course." Although if she had danced with us, I had no memory of that. "And you were there with me when I found Reginleif in the morning. Do you know where you were in between?"

"Everywhere and nowhere," she said, then sort of sang it to herself under her breath. "Everywhere and nowhere and everywhere and nowhere and..."

"Did you see what happened to Reginleif?" I asked.

She sat up straighter and gazed fixedly at me with those half-blind eyes. "Did I see? You mean *see*?"

"Are you talking about prophecy?" I asked, beyond confused. "Can you do that?"

"Can you do that?" she repeated. Although whether she was turning my question around on me or just babbling sounds, it was impossible to tell.

"Njorun," I started to say, but she talked right over me.

"I see. Many things. All things. No things. Who knows things? Reginleif was always going to die. We're all always going to die," she said, her voice dropping into a low, rumbling timber at the end.

"You foresaw her death? What did you see?" I asked, not sure I was understanding her at all.

"Doesn't matter," Njorun said. "Nothing changes. It all goes on and on and on. Always like it was like it was always going to be."

"What's the point of seeing if you can't even warn anybody?" I asked.

"Exactly," she said, then slumped down like a child sulking.

"It's too late to save Reginleif's life, but that doesn't mean the things you saw are useless now," I said. "Can you remember any of it?"

"I knew she knew I knew she knew," she babbled.

"Njorun, can you try to make sense? Just a few sentences?" I asked her. She had managed it briefly before. But now it was like words were just coming out of her, unconnected to anything.

Then she was babbling in the old tongue again. If these words were more relevant than the others, it made no difference. Not if I couldn't understand them.

"Njorun, can you look at me?" I asked helplessly.

"No," she said with sudden clarity.

"Why not?" I asked.

"You're too bright," she said. And she shielded her eyes as if from the sun.

That was alarming. I had been forbidden to leave the boundaries of Villmark for months after I first arrived because I couldn't contain my magic. I literally glowed like a lighthouse, a beacon for those with eyes to see magic. I lured things to me, things drawn by my power. Things that would want to attack or even consume me.

It had taken so long to learn how to contain that glow. But since then, it had become second nature to me. I didn't even think about it anymore.

Which was why Njorun acting like I was blinding her was so distressing. *I had stopped even thinking about it.* Was I once more running around like the most irresistible, impossible-to-miss bait?

I quickly checked myself, but I was not, in fact, glowing.

I looked at Njorun again. She was still flinching away from me, but that childlike think Hulda had mentioned was back in full force.

"Is that all you're going to be able to tell me?" I asked her.

"Yes!" she gushed with great relief, then bolted out of the wagon before I could say another word.

"Knock-knock," Nilda said through the open doorway. She and Kara were standing on the grass just outside the door.

"Come on in," I said, picking up the sleeping Mjolner and setting him back on the bunk behind me. Was he really so tired? Why? Was it from the days of walking we had done? Or was he having nocturnal adventures I knew nothing about?

"Did you learn anything useful?" Kara asked.

"Not really," I admitted. I gave them a quick rundown of what everyone had said, and when I finished, we were all frowning as we looked down at the tabletop between us.

"I don't remember Thorfinna hurting you," Kara said first, touching my forearm gently.

"I don't either," I said. "She was insistent about the mead, but not like that."

"More like any other Villmarker at a party, really," Nilda said. "I didn't feel any malice in it."

"Unless she was very good at pretending to be like any other Villmarker," Kara said. "It's worth remembering that she's the reason we were all out cold the next morning."

"All except Njorun," I said.

"I'm not even remotely ready to try to figure that woman out," Nilda said. "For what it's worth, when I was assisting Yngvildr with the body, I didn't notice anything unusual at all. No pinprick anywhere on the body, and no matter what Hulda says, that would've left a mark. We were very thorough. And Yngvildr was crying the entire time. Not like some display, either. Just genuine tears as she touched her friend for the last time."

"Hulda reminds me of Halldis," I said. "I think that's blinding me to what might really be going on with her."

"Do you sense power from her?" Nilda asked.

"No, but I never did with Halldis either," I said glumly. "Not until it was too late."

"You weren't even really a volva then, though," Kara said. "You're much better at all that now."

"What about you?" I asked.

"No, I don't sense anything. But I haven't been trained to, yet," she said.

"You should start drawing now, right?" Nilda said.

"Yeah," I said. But I didn't get up from the table.

"You should've drawn the murder scene when you found it," Kara said. Not accusingly, just stating a fact.

"I don't have to do it right away for it to show me things," I said. But I knew I sounded sullen.

"No, I know that," she said. But her frown deepened. "It feels like you're dragging your feet about it, though, and I don't understand why."

"Ingrid? Is that true?" Nilda asked me.

I chewed at my lip. I hadn't felt like I was avoiding it, but now that

Kara was mentioning it, I realized I had found excuse after excuse not to start.

"Ingrid?" Kara said when the silence stretched on too long.

"Maybe I'm scared," I admitted. "I don't understand what I feel coming from those stones. And I don't get a sense as to whether they are good or evil. Or friendly or not."

"Does that matter?" Nilda asked.

"Sometimes, when I do this, I get swept up," I said. Those words were so inadequate, but I really didn't want to try to dig up better ones. Just that effort would be so triggering.

"We'll be there with you," Kara said. "And so will Mjolner, right? He's certainly rested up enough. If things go sideways, he'll be there to help me pull you back."

"You're right," I said with a sigh. "I can't put it off anymore. We need to solve this."

"I'll get your stuff," Nilda said and hopped out of the wagon. Mjolner yawned, stretched, then thumped down to the floor to pad after her.

I almost chuckled out loud. Had Kara been right about the reason for his napping? He could've told me.

But Kara, not following her sister back out into the daylight, was giving me a strange look.

"What is it?" I asked.

"What you said. You feel it too," she whispered to me.

"That the Thors still need us? Yes, I have that feeling all the time," I admitted. "Are we wasting our time here?"

I didn't add my other fear, that all of this was happening because someone *wanted* us to waste our time.

But Kara was shaking her head. "No. We still need to do this. For Reginleif. I have this feeling that she died trying to protect someone. Us or Villmark or the Thors, I don't know which. But we can't leave her murder unsolved and her murderer running free."

"I agree," I said. But before she could leave, I caught her up in a tight hug. "I'm glad we're doing this together."

"Me, too," she said, patting my arm. "Now, let's go finish this."
I followed her out the wagon door.

CHAPTER THIRTEEN

THE THREE OF us walked back to the stones. It was midafternoon, and the sun was hot on my skin. I would swear the grass around us had grown in the few days since I had been out here last. Thanks to the funeral rites, there were almost no flowers left among the green blades, although a few buds were striving to take their place.

Then we reached the stones themselves. The grass was starting to recover from whatever had trampled it down in a spiral around the stones, bent stalks straightening and fresh shoots thrusting up through the dried remains of the broken grass. The coppery blood smell was gone from the air, leaving just the cleaner smell of dried grass.

I sat down with my back to the sun and pulled my sketchbook out of my bag. Mjolner curled up beside me, but for once didn't promptly drop off to sleep. He just sat next to me, watching as I took out sticks of charcoal and pencils and turned to a clean page in the book.

"Where do you want us?" Nilda asked.

"Why don't you sit behind me, just out of my field of view," I said. "That way, you'll be close enough to help if I need it without interfering in the drawing."

Without a word, the two of them settled into the grass behind me.

There was a rustling as they sat and arranged themselves, but then they were completely silent. I couldn't even hear them breathing over the buzz of the bees in the grass.

I set the book on my knees, then took up a stick of charcoal. But before touching it to paper, I looked again at the stones in front of me.

I knew it was bees making the buzzing noise, but it was hard to shake the feeling that the stones were buzzing too. Alive with the power within them.

And I was about to poke that power.

Then my hand started moving over the page. The charcoal stick skipped and scraped over the grain of the paper as I drew, first just general patches of light and dark, then more details of the grass.

I was no longer making conscious decisions, just letting the artistic flow take me, when I saw the body taking shape under the charcoal. I caught myself searching already for clues, a sure-fire way to lose the flow in a hurry. I closed my eyes, only for a moment, then resumed the drawing.

Then I lost all sense of time, all awareness of my body hunched over the book, even the sensation of the sun beating down on my back as I worked.

But I was aware of so much more.

It felt like my grandmother was there with me, sitting just beside me on that grass. She wasn't helping with my work, not over that distance. I wasn't even sure if she was aware of me at all, actually. I think I was just sensing her thinking of Reginleif. Somehow, she knew that her friend was dead. And she was grieving.

I really hoped Loke and Roarr were bringing her supplies from town more frequently now that they knew she was alone. I didn't like the thought of her on that lake side by herself, dealing with this grief. I could feel it radiating off her in waves.

I also sensed a little fear. She had sent us to Reginleif so that Reginleif could protect us. Now we were out here alone, unprotected. She was worried about the three of us. I tried to reach out to her, to let her know we were all right. But the minute I tried to do anything besides observe, I broke the spell, and she was gone.

I opened eyes I hadn't realized I had closed to see Kara squatting beside me, her hand on my arm.

"What happened?" I asked. It didn't seem like all that much time had passed. The sun was still high in the sky. But I could feel a prickle on the back of my neck, like the beginning of a sunburn.

"You seemed upset," Kara said. "The stones?"

"No, it was my grandmother," I said. "I sensed her, I think because her thoughts were so focused on Reginleif. She knows she's dead. And now she's worried about us. I tried to reassure her, but before I could, the connection just broke."

"So you didn't get anything from the stones at all?" Kara asked.

I wasn't sure. I looked down at my sketchbook.

Sometimes I woke from a fugue state to find myself drowning in sketches. Once I had used every scrap of paper in my entire house without even realizing it.

But this time I had drawn only one sketch. Not a hastily scrawled thing, though. This was rich with details.

I wondered a little if my subconscious, artistic self was still beating itself up for how well my grandmother had drawn that map. Like it wanted to prove it could work hard, too.

"You drew us too," Kara said, pointing without touching the paper. I had indeed put myself and Mjolner in the foreground, Nilda on one side and Kara on the other.

"I think that means this was definitely about us, somehow," I said. "But also the Thors. See them there, in the grass?"

Unlike the three figures in the foreground, the Thors in the drawing were more of a suggestion of light and shadow in the drawing of the grass. But they were definitely there, all five of them, represented more by their distinctive weapons than by their faces.

"So this is about them, too?" Kara asked.

Nilda crept up on the other side of me so she could see too.

"You didn't draw the stones at all?" she said.

I looked at my drawing again. She was right, sort of. "Look," I pointed out. "I didn't draw them where they actually are, for whatever reason. But I can see their outlines there, within the center of the body."

"What does that mean?" Kara asked.

"Maybe it means Reginleif really was drawing their power," I said. "Or maybe it just means they were connected to her. I still don't really know."

"Do you want to try drawing again?" Kara asked.

"No," I said, but very reluctantly.

I had a hunch what I needed to do next, and it scared me more than the idea of drawing the stones had. And yet, that had turned out not to be anything to be afraid of.

Of course, it hadn't been helpful, either.

"What are you thinking?" Nilda asked me.

"I think I need your knife," I said, nodding towards the knife she kept tucked into her belt opposite her sword. "I have a penknife in this bag somewhere, but I wouldn't attest to its cleanliness."

"Mine's clean," Nilda said, and pulled it out. The blade gleamed in the sunlight.

"Maybe this is a bad idea," Kara said as I took Nilda's knife.

"Mjolner, do you think this is a bad idea?" I asked him.

He meowed noncommittally.

"He says it's fine," I said.

"I don't think that's what he said at all," Nilda said.

"If you're doing this, we should both do this," Kara said, drawing her own knife. It was a match for her sister's. Like their swords, they were forged pairs.

"You're doing what Reginleif did?" Nilda asked. "Is that wise? Isn't that what killed her?"

"No, something else killed her," I said.

"Because she was doing what you're about to do," Nilda said.

"You're here to keep watch," Kara said, already moving closer to the stones.

"What am I watching for? One of the others in the camp?" Nilda asked. "If it's magic, I really can't fight magic."

"Mjolner can," I said. Kara and I crawled across the grass to kneel before the stones. Nilda was standing, hovering uncertainly just outside the circle of once-flattened grass. Mjolner was awake, but still curled up with his head on his paws, watching Kara and me.

"Which stone?" Kara asked. There were three of various sizes, the tallest in the middle, like medal winners at the Olympics. "Should we touch the same or different ones?"

"We'll do it together, at the same time," I said. "Whichever one calls to you. Ready?" I held the blade over my palm, but hesitated.

I used my hands a lot. Even paper cuts were irritating when I worked in charcoal. What was this going to do?

"Keep it shallow," Kara said, as if reading my mind. "Just enough to bleed. You won't need to apply any pressure. That blade is sharp enough on its own."

"Right," I said grimly. Then, before I could lose my nerve again, I touched that blade to the skin of my palm.

My first impression was that the blade was strangely cool, a startling contrast to the heat from the sun.

Then I felt the skin split and was so grateful for Kara's words. Left on my own, I would've sliced into my hand like I was chopping onions. And that would've been an overkill I know I would've regretted.

I heard Kara suck in a breath and knew she was bleeding now, too. I looked up at her, and she gave me a nod. Then we both touched one of the stones.

Neither of us touched the tall one in the center, the one Reginleif had touched. I found myself touching the smallest of the three, rubbing the scant blood from my palm over the sun-warm surface. Kara did the same with the middle-sized stone on the far end.

At first, it was like the stone was some sort of sponge, soaking up the blood without a trace. But I flexed my hand, bringing forth a fresh flow of blood, and touched it again. This time, as I wiped my palm over its surface, something appeared. It might have been writing of some sort, but they looked nothing like the runes I knew. It might have just been some sort of drawing, but all the definition had faded with time.

All the color of my blood brought out was rough blobs. But I knew it meant something.

Then I felt a tingling in my arm, and it was like my palm was stuck to the stone, pressing hard against the surface. That tingling rushed out of me, into the stone. It was like standing up too fast, when all the blood rushes out of your head, only it was my whole body.

It was rather like what I thought being drained by a vampire would feel like.

But then, just when I was sure I was going to faint, it all rushed back into me again. All the vitality I had lost, and then some.

And it kept coming. And I still couldn't let the stone go.

I looked over at Kara. I was sure her face was a match for mine: filled with wonder but also fear. I could see her trying to pull her hand free, but like mine, it was stuck there.

Then I saw a golden light emanating from the stone, filling my hand and then up my arm to fill my body. It was just like the light that had glowed from Reginleif when we had all danced under the stars.

I could feel her all around me. I could smell the herby smell of the inside of her wagon, but ten times as strong.

Then I fell back onto the grass, my hand finally free. And I heard Kara tumbling over on the other side of the stones.

"What was that?" Kara asked me. She was breathing hard, like she'd just run a mile.

I was breathing hard myself, but I had never in my life felt so exhilarated.

"I think that was Reginleif," I said. "That missing piece of her. It's in us now. Whatever that means."

Kara closed her eyes, turning her awareness within. "I don't remember any of her memories. I don't know what happened to her here."

"Me neither," I said after scanning my own mind. "But something is different. I feel different."

"Do you want to try drawing again?" Nilda asked. I looked over at her, still watching over us. Mjolner beside her was slipping in and out of a doze, his cat eyes blinking towards sleep.

"Not here," I decided. "I think we've learned all we can here."

"Which was nothing," Kara said, getting up from the grass and dusting off the back of her pants. She picked up her knife, then took out a rag from her pocket to polish it clean.

"We're not done yet," I told her.

I was feeling supremely confident. Probably because I still felt like I was glowing with that golden light. It was like I was filled with power. But I didn't know what I could do with it.

I thought of my grandmother alone in the cabin, and for just a fraction of a second, it was like she thought of me too. Our minds touched, then parted.

But she knew we were okay. Even in that brief contact, I sensed some of her fear had lessened.

Then I tried to do the same again, this time with Thorbjorn. But apparently, this trick needed a location to work properly. My mind knew where to find my grandmother, but I had no idea where Thorbjorn was.

Or maybe it was because, unlike my grandmother, Thorbjorn was not a user of magic. Maybe the communication had to go both ways to work.

I pushed away a third possibility, that he hadn't responded to me because he couldn't. Because he wasn't there at all. But even not thinking about it, I still felt an emptiness. Like he was gone to me.

"We'll find them," Kara said, and took my injured hand in hers. There was a little jolt, like static electricity between us, and she smiled.

"I know," I said. "But, the killer first."

"The killer first," she agreed.

Then Nilda wrapped both of our hands in clean bandages she took from the pouch on her belt. My hand had already stopped bleeding, but moving it too much would likely get it going again.

Which would be a problem, because I knew I had more drawing to do.

CHAPTER FOURTEEN

WHEN WE GOT BACK to the campsite under the tree, we found the others had built up a smaller fire a little distance away from the remains of the bonfire. A cast-iron pot hung from an iron tripod, flames licking its rounded bottom, but all that seemed to be inside of it so far was water that had not yet come to a boil.

Thorfinna had a small stack of dead rabbits on a table just outside of her wagon and was in the process of dressing them. I felt something brush against my leg as Mjolner shot away from the three of us to give Thorfinna all of his most worshipful attention.

Hulda was washing shriveled-looking potatoes in a basin just outside her own tent, and Yngvildr emerged from hers with fistfuls of fresh green herbs.

Rabbit stew for dinner, then, but not for at least another hour. My stomach grumbled loudly. My breakfast had been a bit of our travel food, jerky and dried fruit with some nuts, and I had skipped lunch entirely. I didn't think the blood loss was making me lightheaded, but the strain of even the little magic I used when drawing was telling. I needed food.

"Reginleif has some cheese in her wagon," Kara said. "That should tide us over."

"You're feeling it too?" I said, and she nodded. "I thought it was from the drawing. I guess the stones took something out of us."

"They gave more back, but not the same thing," Kara said. "I'm starving."

"Well met, Torfudottir and the Mikkelsens!" Thorfinna called to us, waving a bloody hand in the air. "We're making dinner. What have you been up to?"

"I was drawing the murder scene," I said. Hulda was dropping her potatoes into the water one by one, but I sensed her listening intently. Yngvildr had stopped in front of me with those herbs still in her hands.

"Can we see?" she asked. "Is that allowed?"

"I don't see why not," I said. I sat down on one of the stools near the campfire and took my sketchbook out of my bag. I turned to the correct page and looked over my drawing again. There were so many details there I still hadn't examined properly. Every line served two functions, it seemed like.

Yngvildr moved around to stand over my shoulder. "Oh, look! Just around the body. In the grass. Don't you see?"

I looked. There were flowering plants flattened down with the grass that I hadn't noticed before.

"Do you know what they are?" I asked her. Judging from her reaction to seeing them, they had to mean something.

"Those are purple coneflowers," she said. "It's too soon for them to be blooming, though. I didn't notice any when we were out there cleaning up her body. And yet you drew them there all around her."

"Does it have some kind of significance?" I asked. I was thinking of Ophelia's dialogue in Hamlet, the meaning of all the flowers. Rosemary for remembrance, pansies for thoughts. Every flower meant something, didn't it?

"Oh, I only mention it because the last time I saw Reginleif before meeting here for the Dísablót, she had asked me if I had any on hand," Yngvildr said. "The dried roots have strong medicinal value. I gave her as much as I could spare. But I didn't ask why she wanted them. It looks from your drawing that she wanted them for herself, maybe, and not to give to someone else. Doesn't it look like they sprout out of her body?"

I looked at the picture again. It did kind of look like that. But I didn't know what that could tell me. "Isn't that just echinacea? Like for colds?" I asked her.

"I don't know that name," she said. Which made sense. I didn't know Villmarker Norse for it, so I had just used the Greek name. Terribly common in the modern world, but pretty much unknown here. "It has many uses."

I looked at the drawing again, but nothing was jumping out at me. Not with the flowers, or with anything else either. Usually there was something that caught my eye, that led me to a clue. But this was just a drawing. I didn't need to be in a fugue state to draw something like what I was holding now.

"May I see it?" Thorfinna asked. She was wiping her hands dry on a towel after washing the blood from them, and I handed her the book. She looked it over closely. "You've captured them well, haven't you? The Thors."

"I don't see them," Yngvildr said.

"They're just there," Thorfinna said impatiently, pointing with one enormous finger. "The weapons are larger; their individual faces are worked into the weapons. And it's all hidden in the grass."

"I guess I see it," Yngvildr said, but with the air of someone who doesn't want to admit they can't see the sailboat in the magic eye drawing. She turned away to find a wooden bowl to put her handfuls of herbs in.

"It's very clever," Thorfinna said. I shrugged off the praise, my artist self being pathologically incapable of dealing with anything like that. But she scowled at me, and I realized I had missed her meaning.

"It's just their faces and their weapons," I said.

"But they are there, part of the scene, and yet apart from it," Thorfinna said. "They almost looked trapped there, in that grass. Don't they?"

That piqued Kara's interest. Now she was hovering over Thorfinna's elbow to look herself.

"They do look like they're being held back," she said, looking up at me.

"Something is keeping them away from us," I said. Not adding that vice versa also felt true.

"May I?" Hulda asked. She sounded thoroughly uninterested, only being polite. She clearly didn't care enough to try to peek over Thorfinna's elbows, although she wasn't that much shorter, really. She just held out her hand until Thorfinna reluctantly handed the book over.

"Do you see anything we missed?" I asked after too long of a silence. She didn't answer right away, just kept scanning the image again and again, searching the details.

"It doesn't seem to help solve the murder," Thorfinna said almost apologetically. Like she was the one who had drawn it. Then she turned and picked up the bowl overflowing with chopped rabbit meat and carried it over to the now boiling pot.

Mjolner was licking his lips. He had gotten something while everyone's attention had been away.

"I agree. It doesn't solve anything," Hulda said, and turned towards the fire with the book in her hands.

For one horrifying moment, I thought she was going to toss the whole thing into the fire. The loss of that sketch was bad enough, but the rest of the book was filled with everything I had seen on the walk from the cabin to the meadow. Days and days of sketches. Mundane sketches done in a hurry while in a state of exhaustion, camping at the side of the road, but still.

The fire flared up with snaps and crackles, but when Hulda turned away and walked back to her tent, I saw that Njorun had been standing behind her. The old woman had my sketchbook now and took it with her to sit on one of the other stools.

She was cackling and chatting with herself in that language that none of us seemed to understand. She touched the page, something no one else had done, but gently, only barely smearing the charcoal on the paper.

"Do you see anything there, Njorun?" I asked her. It was an effort not to speak to her in the pitch and cadence that one used with a child. I had always hated when anyone talked to older people like that. It was so condescending.

And yet that childlike quality Njorun always had felt like it had regressed to full babyhood. She was like an infant whose eyes could only focus on black and white images, babbling away as they looked at a high contrast drawing of a butterfly.

"She sounds happy about what she sees, anyway," Kara said to me.

"She does," I agreed. Somehow, that made my heart feel lighter.

"You know what you should do?" Thorfinna said as she washed her hands clean for a second time. "You should draw again."

"I don't think that would help," I said. "I saw everything there was to see the first time."

"Here," Yngvildr said, suddenly squatting at my side and seizing my bandaged hand. She examined the cut, tisked, then spread a greenish salve over it before winding it back up again in clean bandages. Then she straightened up and said to Thorfinna, "she can draw in the morning. That needs time to heal."

"Foolishness, that was," Thorfinna grumbled as Yngvildr went over to do the same to Kara's hand.

"I don't think so," I said, but she was already shaking her head.

"We can all see it. That bit of Reginleif in the two of you," she said, to my surprise.

"You can?"

"You glow, dear," Hulda said as she stood with one hand on her hip, the other stirring at the bubbling stew.

"Anyway, when I said you should draw again, I meant draw each of us," Thorfinna said. "Won't that tell you who's lying and who's telling you the truth?"

Nilda flushed red, and I knew at once where Thorfinna had gotten that impression from.

"Sometimes," I allowed.

"But not until morning," Yngvildr reiterated. "Food and rest first. Drawing after."

"And you should sleep in the wagon, dear," Hulda said to me. "That's what your cat has been trying to tell you."

I doubted that was what Mjolner meant at all, but I didn't argue. As small as that bunk in the wagon was, after days of sleeping on the ground, it would feel finer than any California king.

"We'll keep watch," Nilda said, and Kara nodded.

"Are you sure?" I asked.

"Drawing is not my thing," Kara said. "I guess I don't know what my thing is. In the meantime, keeping watch is something I can do."

"Very well," I said.

My stomach grumbled again, but Yngvildr was there, pressing a wrinkled apple into my hands. "To tide you over," she whispered to me.

"I'll get the cheese," Kara said, as she took her own apple from the bowl in Yngvildr's arms.

Thorfinna settled onto the stool next to mine with an exaggerated sigh, then just stared at the fire as if she could will it to cook the stew faster.

"Thorfinna?" I said, and she glanced over at me expectantly. "If the Thors really are trapped somewhere, do you have any idea where we should start looking?"

"Something that would trap the Thors," she said, tapping her steepled fingers on her chin thoughtfully. "I have a few ideas."

"Could you draw us a map?" I asked. "Or even just point out likely places on my grandmother's map?"

"I can do better than that," she said with a lopsided grin. "When this is all over and we're free to go, I'll show you all those places myself."

"I'm sure that's not necessary—" I started to say, but she cut me off with a single raised hand.

"Please, Torfudottir. If you don't take me with you, I'll just follow you myself. No one is going to rest until they are found, least of all me."

"Thank you," I said.

"Thank me when they're found," she said, and turned her attention back to the fire.

Reginleif had told us someone at the Dísablót would be able to help us find the Thors. And she had brought us to Thorfinna first.

Maybe that had meant something.

I could only hope.

CHAPTER FIFTEEN

I WOKE in the morning on that bunk feeling ridiculously refreshed. Mjolner even seemed in brighter spirits, stretching and yawning before curling up again on the bit of pillow where my head had just been.

Then I stepped out of the wagon and felt a twinge of guilt. Nilda and Kara were both awake, sitting together by the fire. I could smell the coffee from where I was and wondered where they had gotten it. We hadn't brought any with us. The closest to bickering any of us had done on our long hike had been focused around just whose oversight that was.

"Good morning, dear," Hulda said as she emerged from her tent. Not only was she already dressed, her hair was arranged in a braided crown, two pins like gold circles holding the braids in place behind her ears. A very elaborate hairdo. Just how early had *she* been up? It was barely an hour after dawn, the grass still damp from the dew.

"Good morning," I said, adding an extra smile of thanks when Nilda handed me a mug of coffee.

"I have pan bread as well," Hulda said, holding out a cast-iron skillet filled with a lumpy golden mass. A few lumps had already been taken.

"It's really good," Kara said. Clearly, it hurt her a little to admit that.

"I'm an excellent cook," Hulda said. "And also provider of things."

"It's her coffee," Nilda admitted.

"I have more than enough to share. I just didn't realize you all were doing without," she said as I helped myself to a chunk of her bread. It was oily on the bottom, to keep it from sticking to the pan. The tops were crusty brown, but the center was still warm and chewy.

"Wow," I said. "This is fantastic."

"Thorfinna cooks bacon in her pan first and then the bread. Which is divine, only she wakes up so late," Hulda said. "Mine's just olive oil."

"Where do you get olive oil and coffee?" I asked her.

"Trade," she said with a shrug. As if that answered anything. It actually led to a bunch more questions, like just how many people were there in the north and where did they all come from? But she didn't give me an opportunity to swallow the bread in my mouth to ask before going on. "I was thinking since I'm the only one up yet, maybe you could draw me first? If you're ready, that is. How's your hand?"

"Better," I said, although I hadn't even looked at it yet. I unwound the bandage, then went to the pail of water near the remains of the campfire to wash the green salve away. When I was done, there was only a slightly pink line across my palm. The cut had healed closed already and looked like it would soon fade without leaving a scar.

I flexed and closed my hand a few times, but the skin moved without a twinge of pain.

"Do you want to go into your wagon?" Hulda asked me.

"No, let's do it outside," I said. I reached into the wagon for my art bag, then sat on one of the stools by the campfire. Hulda sat on an upended log close by, arranging her skirts, then throwing back her shoulders in an artful pose.

I wanted to tell her it wasn't going to be that kind of portrait. Then I realized I was reaching for my pencils, not my charcoal. Charcoal was my usual choice for magic drawing, since I worked so much faster with it, especially in rudimentary sketches. Pencils gave me more fine control, but without the speed of process, it was harder to get into that fugue state.

And yet, this was no time to be questioning my subconscious impulses. I stuck with the pencils.

Hulda held her pose without complaint, only occasionally brushing back a strand of hair when the breeze tangled it into her eyelashes or it stuck to the corner of her mouth. I could hear Nilda and Kara murmuring together somewhere behind me, but not intrusively. Yngvildr and Thorfinna were so quiet I assumed they were still sleeping.

I sketched Hulda's outlines in a fine pencil, then switched to a darker, thicker pencil to start working the details. I was engrossed, but this was an artistic sort of state. Not the magical fugue state I had been hoping for.

I set my pencil down with a sigh, looking at what I had drawn so far. It was good, as far as portraits went. Even unfinished, I could see that. But there were no clues lurking in the details.

"Everything going all right?" Hulda asked, still holding her pose, her fingers threaded together as she clasped one knee loosely.

"Fine," I said, a bit shortly.

"I've not seen this sort of magic done before," she said. "It seems very interesting. But I would think you would glow more while you were doing it."

"You can see magic like that?" I asked skeptically.

"Of course," she said. "I know my powers are small, but seeing things is easy enough. You keep your magic tamped down hard, but there are still gleams to be seen, especially when we're as close as the two of us are now."

"And you can tell when I'm attempting something magical?" I asked.

"Well, I wasn't there when you drew that last sketch," she admitted. "But during the Dísablót, you were quite bright to look at. Not quite like Reginleif, but unmistakably a user of magic."

"And you don't see that now?" I asked.

She broke her pose enough to glance over at me, then gave me an almost apologetic shake of the head.

"Sorry, dear. No," she said. "But maybe you just need to try a different approach?"

"Maybe I should start again with charcoal," I said, looking at my bag at my feet. But I made no move to reach for those pencils.

"Or—and I know this is just a suggestion from an amateur, so feel free to disregard it entirely—maybe you should try getting in touch with your magic first? And then draw?"

"That might work," I admitted.

"I'll be still now," Hulda said, and resumed the perfect posture of her pose.

I closed my eyes and let my awareness spread around me. I could hear the bees humming through the grass, the whisper of the breeze rustling those blades together, the occasional crackle from the embers of the dying fire. I could smell the pan bread, especially the olive oil, still lingering on the air even more than the smell of the wood and ash. I could feel the sun on my skin, prickly on the back of my neck where I had started to burn the day before.

The hum of the bees grew louder until it was everything around me. I only existed inside of that humming.

Then someone shook my shoulder hard enough to spill me off of the stool. I put out a hand to catch myself before hitting the ground, then looked up to see Nilda standing over me.

"Sorry," she said. "I tried just slapping you first."

No wonder my cheek felt hot and tingly. "That was your first impulse?" I said.

"Well, after calling your name and just generally shaking you. But you're back now. Finally."

"What happened?" I asked, climbing back onto the stool. I touched the hot spot on my cheek, then saw my sketchbook laying on the ground. I picked it up and brushed it off, then turned to the page I had been working on before.

The sketch of Hulda was half-finished. I had added nothing while in that fugue state.

I looked up at the log, but Hulda was no longer there.

"What happened?" I asked again.

"You were catatonic when we found you," Nilda said, but I was no longer listening.

"Give me a minute," I said, scrambling through my bag for my charcoals. I turned the page and started drawing again, so furiously I kept breaking the ends off my fragile charcoal pencils. I switched to my woodless ones and drew on.

When I finally stopped and looked up again, Nilda and Kara both were standing over me. It was high noon now, although how much of that time had passed while I was drawing in charcoal and how much had passed before, when I had apparently just been sitting there, I couldn't tell.

"Hulda disappeared," Kara told me. "She was chatting with you, and you were drawing, so Nilda and I went back towards the forest to do a little hunting. We came back with a few more rabbits to find you on the ground, and Hulda gone. Tent and all."

"She had enough time to pack?" I asked, my voice a tad too shrill.

"Well, we assumed that was magic," Nilda said.

I looked down at the drawing in my hands. Hulda was there, sitting on the log like she was supposed to be. But the lines of the tree behind her seemed to be connected to her. Like she was webbed to its branches. Not unlike how the Thors had been webbed into the grass in my other sketch.

"You drew us," Kara said, even as I shifted my attention to the far corner of the sketch, where the three of us were crowded together.

At first, it was hard to tell what was going on with our figures. Charcoal adds darkness, layer after layer. But the layers here were lighter and smudged down to the paper in several places by my own fingertips.

"We're glowing," I said, touching the page with my darkened fingers.

"What does that mean?" Kara asked. "Is it because of the stones?"

"I would think so, except it's clearly coming from Nilda too. And she never touched the stones." I looked up at her to make sure this was still true, and she shook her head. She hadn't done the ritual without us.

"Where did Hulda go?" I asked.

"Thorfinna took her horse and is looking for her now," Kara said. "But there was no trail that any of us can see. It's just like she lifted up into the sky."

"If you two saw no trail, then there was no trail," I said with certainty. They were two of the best hunters in Villmark. That meant this had to be magic.

And yet Hulda hadn't seemed capable of it. Was she that good at pretending? Or was something else going on here?

I touched the page again, this time where the lines connected her to the tree.

I got up and walked over to the tree. I pressed my hands to the bark, but felt nothing. The tree was old, and living, I felt that. But it had no magic.

I had seen something when I had drawn that webbing. But maybe I hadn't understood exactly what I had seen. Not being aware of anything when I was actually producing these drawings was a bit of a drawback. But I knew the Thors weren't literally in the grass either. So the webby textures had to mean something else.

But I was pretty sure they were connected.

I just didn't know how.

CHAPTER SIXTEEN

I DIDN'T EXACTLY GO BACK into a fugue state, but I did stop paying attention to the world around me for a bit. Nilda and Kara's voices were once more mere murmuring in the background. The sun was still hot, but now at an angle that didn't beat down on the blistering skin of my neck.

I worked extra hard to tune out the buzzing of the bees.

But mostly I just focused on that drawing of Hulda. Was there any clue there that she was the one who had killed Reginleif?

If there was, I didn't see it. She looked more like a victim herself, caught by surprise by whatever was emanating from that tree.

I might have been projecting a little, but I was willing to consider that as cancelling out my general distrust of Hulda because she reminded me of Halldis.

But what did that leave me with? Just a sense of a woman I didn't know at all, really.

Certainly, if she had any motive to kill Reginleif, I had caught no hint of it.

I finally looked up when Thorfinna blustered back into camp, leading her horse and carrying another four or five rabbits tied together by their back feet in her other hand.

"At least it wasn't a total waste of time," she said as she slammed the rabbits down on her butchering table.

"We have a few as well," Kara told her. "Shame no one seems to be hungry."

"I'm angry enough to eat," Thorfinna growled, but made no move to build up the fire.

"You know who else is missing? Yngvildr," Nilda said. "Kara and I were looking for her out in the meadow, but there's no sign of her."

"Her tent is still here," I said.

"And we saw her this morning. But that was before Hulda disappeared," Kara said.

Thorfinna scowled even more fiercely. "So, did they run off together or is this some fresh problem to be solved?"

"Did you see her this morning?" I asked Thorfinna.

"I did not," Thorfinna said, still vexed. Then she softened a little to add, "your friends woke me up to look for Hulda. I didn't even ask who else was searching, but I assumed when I didn't see Yngvildr that she had already been put on the task."

"No, we couldn't find her then," Kara said.

"We assumed she was gathering plants nearby, but we didn't look," Nilda admitted. "But she didn't come back for lunch, so we started to wonder about it. We've been all over the meadow from waterfall to waterfall, but there's no sign of her."

"I'll check her tent," I said, getting up from the stool with my sketchbook and charcoal pencils in hand.

"She's not there," Nilda told me.

"I know," I said, and slipped between the flaps. The interior was almost entirely given over to basket after basket of gathered plants. More plants hung from lines strung across the top of the tent, drying in the warm interior as the sun beat down on the canvas. Almost unseen in the corner was a narrow little cot.

I sat down in the doorway where I could see everything and put my book on my knees.

To my relief, my block from the morning was completely gone now. Part of my mind wanted to wonder if Hulda had caused that somehow, but most of my mind was focused on my hands furiously scratching charcoal all over the page. I drew quickly, but when I was done, the image was clearly the interior of the tent before me. I had drawn the plants in surprising detail, things I hadn't even realized I had noticed about the shapes of their leaves and flowers.

But one plant in particular caught my attention. It was within a vial that was inside of a chest that was tucked under the cot. But I had drawn its shape in heavy, sure lines.

"Anyone recognize this plant?" I asked as I came out of the tent to show the others my drawing. My hands were nearly all black by now, covered in charcoal. Kara took the book from me and the other two gathered around her while I went to the pail by the fire to wash my hands.

"No," Nilda said, looking at Kara, who also shook her head.

"You know who would know?" Thorfinna said with dry humor. "Yngvildr."

"She must be planning to come back," I said. "All of her stuff is here. There are a lot of plants in the process of drying in there. I don't see her leaving all that behind."

"Unless she was trying to get away with murder," Thorfinna said darkly.

"What's this?" Kara asked, looking at something in the background of the drawing. I came over to see for myself.

The plant I had drawn most darkly was under the cot, in the corner of the tent. But I had also drawn a bit of the exterior of the tent, even though I hadn't been able to see it from where I was sitting. I had drawn the meadows around the tent, the campfire, and Thorfinna's wagon.

A very faint line connected that plant to Thorfinna's wagon, or to something inside Thorfinna's wagon. I would almost think it meant nothing, but leaving a line with no tone to it at all—a white line like this one—in a charcoal drawing was so technically demanding it had to be deliberate.

"Thorfinna, may I have permission to draw the interior of your wagon?" I asked her gingerly.

"Of course!" she said, so forcefully that all three of us flinched. I was just glad I wasn't the only one who felt blown back by the power of her voice.

She walked me to her wagon and made a show of opening the door for me. I stepped up into the dark space, but Thorfinna went around the outside, opening a series of little shutters, revealing tiny windows. It wasn't much, but it was enough light to see by.

It was the same size as Reginleif's wagon, but where Reginleif's wagon was filled with objects of daily living and had a cozy, homey feel, Thorfinna's was bare and downright spartan. It was all one boxy space, with a pile of furs in one corner to serve as a bed. A box by the door held a single plate and bowl and a very medieval-looking fork. I supposed the cauldron still hanging over the fire would also go there when not in use.

A single chest sat at the foot of the bed of furs, but the lid was open. I could see only a single spare shirt tucked in there. The rest was an assortment of weapons, small throwing knives and axes, and an unmatched set of darts.

I sat down in the doorway, at the very edge of the back of the wagon, and turned to a fresh page. Again I found the drawing came easily, and I soon was looking down at a finished sketch of the interior.

With a fine white line leading to that chest.

"Thorfinna, may I examine the contents of that chest?" I called.

"Help yourself," she said, followed by a loud chopping sound. She was dressing her rabbits, apparently. I crawled further into the wagon and looked inside that chest.

And found the exact knife that Hulda had described to me, the one with a blade as fine as a needle. I carried it with me back out into the sunlight. Thorfinna looked up at me with a single cocked brow but made no move to stop me as I drew the blade out of its scabbard.

There was no blood on it. But there was *something* on that blade. I squinted at it, then held it up into the sunlight to try to get a better look.

This got Thorfinna's attention, and she came closer to look herself.

"Forgot I had that," she mumbled.

"What's that on the blade?" I asked.

"May I take it?" she asked, holding out her meaty hands. I placed the delicate weapon on her palms. It felt so horribly mismatched to those hands the size of bear paws. And yet she hadn't denied it was hers.

"Something corroded the metal," she said with a frown.

"When did you use it last?" I asked.

"I don't recall ever using it," she said. "I won it in a bet. Don't know how long ago. Probably decades, by your reckoning. But what am I going to do with a blade like this? Besides give it to a child to train with."

"My drawing connects that to the plant in Yngvildr's tent," I told her.

Nilda and Kara drew closer. Now both of them were resting their hands on the hilts of their swords. I swallowed, my throat suddenly dry.

I really hoped this wasn't about to become a sword fight. Because even two on one, I didn't like their chances against Thorfinna.

"Hulda told me you had this," I said.

"Hulda did?" Thorfinna said. She certainly seemed genuinely puzzled. "How on Earth would she know?"

"She also said she was up the night of the Dísablót to do some little ceremony, and yet you told me you knew she was sleeping all that night," I said.

Thorfinna frowned, then shrugged. "I don't know what to tell you, Ingrid Torfudottir. As unrivaled as I am at holding my mead, we did have quite a lot of it. When I was out for the night, I was out for the night. She was in her tent when I passed out, and she was there again when I woke. My apologies for making assumptions about everything in between."

"This doesn't really implicate Hulda, though, does it?" Kara said. "Isn't Yngvildr the suspicious one? If she had some killing plant in her tent, but she told us she didn't."

"Maybe she didn't know, or didn't remember," Nilda said. "Like Thorfinna with this blade."

"I had forgotten all about it," Thorfinna said emphatically.

But I looked at Nilda. "You really believe Yngvildr is innocent?" I asked. The two of them had spent the most time together, and that while dealing directly with the body of the victim. If ever there was a moment for someone's mask to slip, that would be it. And I would trust Nilda to notice.

But after thinking it over, Nilda sighed dejectedly. "I don't know. I want to say I trust her, but maybe that trust is misplaced."

"There is the pesky fact that she's missing now," Kara added.

"I looked everywhere for Hulda," Thorfinna said. "And I saw no sign of either of them. Perhaps the two of them were just… taken up into the sky somehow?"

I instantly thought of helicopters hovering low while soldiers jumped on or off. But that would've been loud. We would've noticed.

And Thorfinna was obviously thinking of something else. Something more magical.

Only I should've noticed that as well.

Except I had been in that unproductive fugue state. Which I still wasn't entirely certain hadn't been something Hulda had done to me.

"If they both went together, why did they take Hulda's tent and not Yngvildr's?" Kara asked. "Especially since Yngvildr's tent left us with a clue."

"Maybe Hulda's tent had even more clues," I said glumly. "I should've been drawing that instead of her."

I felt something pressing up against my calf and looked down to see Mjolner rubbing up against my leg, trying to get my attention. I picked him up and scratched around his ears, but he just looked back over my shoulder and meowed insistently.

We all turned to see a figure approaching us through the grass. All dressed in white, with a large veiled hat rather like what beekeepers wear. As the figure came closer, we saw it was a woman, a woman carrying a basket overloaded with greenery. It was so heavy she had both arms looped through the handles and was walking in a limping sort of way, dragged down by the weight.

None of us said a word, although Thorfinna too was now standing with her hand on her sword. I put down Mjolner, then moved closer to the campfire and found my art bag, trading out my sketchbook for my bronze wand.

Not that I knew what I would do with that, exactly. But it felt better not being the only one with nothing in my hands except a cat.

The figure saw us all standing there, our stances more aggressive than strictly defensive, and drew up short. Then she threw back her veil, knocking the entire hat off her head in the process.

It was Yngvildr. She dropped the heavy basket and stumbled a step or two backwards, hands raised.

"What's going on?" she asked. "Why are you all looking at me like that?"

Her hands were trembling even as she held them aloft, and her eyes were wide and frightened.

I just wasn't sure I believed any of it.

CHAPTER SEVENTEEN

I WASN'T the only one less than convinced by Yngvildr's expression of shock and surprise. And she could tell.

She gestured to the baskets at her feet. "I was collecting spring plants. It's what I do every year after the Dísablót ends. I missed two days already, and you didn't seem to need me…"

No one answered her, and she trailed off uncertainly. She looked like she was about to cry.

"We searched the entire meadow. There was no sign of you," Nilda told her, her voice hard.

"I searched the hills and the woods," Thorfinna said. "Didn't see you."

"I was at the top of the waterfalls," Yngvildr said. Then she knelt down beside her basket. "Look, I'll show you. See these mosses? They grow on the south-most waterfall, on the rocks where the sun doesn't reach. Not down here, but up at the top."

"You climbed up there?" Kara asked her skeptically.

"I climb all sorts of places," Yngvildr said defensively. She thrust out a foot, and we saw that she was wearing modern footwear, sneakers in bright colors. Then I realized these weren't running or basketball shoes. The soles were too flexible, and the pads on the bottoms were clearly designed to cling and not slip, especially at the toes. I had never been bouldering myself, but I was sure these were the shoes that people who did tended to wear.

No matter how deep into the wilds I went, no matter how much magic was all around me, artifacts from the modern world were always right there. There was no escaping it.

"I'm sorry for the confusion," Yngvildr said. "I saw you on your horse out by the forest, but I didn't think anything of it," she added to Thorfinna. "I had no idea you were looking for me."

"Actually, I was looking for Hulda," Thorfinna said.

"Hulda?" Yngvildr said, then notice the missing tent. "She just packed up and left?"

"She disappeared, and all her stuff, but packing up and hiking out doesn't seem to have been her method," I said.

"What ever is going on?" Yngvildr said.

"I have a better question," I said, and put my wand away to take out my sketchbook once more. I showed her the drawing of her tent and pointed at the plant, as if she could possibly miss noticing it. "What is this?"

"What is that?" she repeated, taking the book from me. I watched as all the color drained from her face. "That looks like… well, the only name I know for it is bani," she said. A Norse word.

"Doesn't that just mean, like, poison?" I asked.

She nodded miserably, setting the book aside as if she wanted it very far from her. "It's very rare, but very deadly."

"And when we asked if you knew anything that could kill Reginleif without a sign, you didn't mention this?" Thorfinna asked her in a growl.

"I didn't even know I had it," she said. "But the way you drew it, in that chest under my cot, I remember it now. It was part of a set of unlabeled vials I found in an abandoned village—"

"Let me guess," I interrupted. "Years ago?"

"Yes!" she insisted. "It took me years just to identify what was in those vials. The other two were also poisons, if less deadly. The other two I threw away. Diluted in the waters of the lake, they were no harm to any living thing. But bani? Even diluted, it would harm creatures. And it would harm anyone who ate of those creatures."

"It sounds very potent," I said.

"It *is*," she said. "I was going to bury it, bury it deep in some barren place. But I guess I forgot," she finished lamely.

"I believe her," Nilda said suddenly, to everyone's surprise, but no one's more than Yngvildr.

"Why?" I asked.

"It's too much like what Thorfinna said. She had that blade she didn't remember having," Nilda said. "The only thing that would make the picture more complete was if Hulda had told you it was there when you interviewed her."

"No, she didn't mention it," I said.

"Bani would leave no sign that I would've seen without cutting into the body, which I didn't want to do," Yngvildr said. "But there were other signs, signs I missed."

"Such as?" I asked.

"The clotting of the blood on Reginleif's palm," she said. "It had clotted and sealed before she died. But it would've been freely bleeding still when she was stabbed, wouldn't it?"

"If our idea of what happened there is correct," I said.

"That would be in keeping with the effects of bani," she said. "It clots the blood and hardens the organs. I didn't see the latter without cutting into her, as I said. But it also would've clotted and sealed the wound that delivered the poison. Even more so, so close to the source."

"That's why we didn't see it," Nilda guessed.

"I think so," Yngvildr said.

We all lapsed into silence, each lost in our own thoughts. Then suddenly, Kara sucked in a breath. We all looked at her in alarm, and she flushed, but then she said, "I don't know how we all missed it, but Njorun is missing too."

I rubbed tiredly at my forehead. I couldn't recall seeing her at all that day. And she more than anyone I could see just lifting up into the sky, as light as she was.

"Did any of us see her?" Thorfinna asked.

"Not even when we were looking for Yngvildr," Nilda said.

"Same when I was searching for Hulda," Thorfinna said. I think she was about to say something more, but Mjolner, who had left my arms some time ago to nap in a sunny patch of meadow, gave a sudden sleepy meow.

The others looked at the cat, but I looked the other way, where his half-closed eyes had been directed.

Njorun was there, sitting in grass so tall it nearly hid her, the blades curving over her head like a tipi. She had my sketchbook on her lap and was looking at the pages and chattering to herself.

Then she looked up and fixed me with those cloudy eyes, and her entire demeanor changed. Gone was the childlike quality. Now she was all earnestness, jabbing at the drawings and saying something over and over again. They were definitely words, intelligible to somebody. But not to me.

"It's older Norse than I know," Thorfinna said before I could even ask.

"I never understand her," Yngvildr said. "But she's definitely trying to show you something about that drawing."

I walked over to crouch beside Njorun. I could smell the mustiness of her clothes and her unwashed body beneath it.

"What is it?" I asked her.

But she could summon no words I knew. She sighed at my lack of understanding and turned the page to jab at the drawing of Thorfinna's wagon, but I still had no idea what she meant.

"We know the plant and the blade are connected," I told her. "That's what the white line meant. But I'm sorry, I'm not seeing anything new here."

Njorun jabbed a few more times, then gave up, her entire body slumping in defeat.

I took the book from her lap and stood up. Then I bent over her, offering her a hand. She took it, allowing me to pull her to her feet.

She weighed nothing at all. I was only worried that I didn't squeeze her hand too tightly. Those bird bones would snap like dried twigs if I weren't careful.

"What are you going to do now?" Yngvildr asked.

"Njorun has no tent or wagon," I said. "And as much as I had no luck drawing Hulda herself, I don't see another option here. I'm going to try drawing Njorun herself."

"She certainly seems to know something," Thorfinna said. "Is it going to be distracting if I finish with these rabbits and get some of them roasting on a spit?"

"No, and the food will be most welcome," I told her. "Njorun and I will go inside Reginleif's wagon. She seemed receptive to that space."

"Do you need anyone to watch over you?" Kara asked.

"No, I should be all right," I said as I fetched my art bag. But when I climbed into the wagon, I realized I wasn't going to be alone in there with this strange woman.

Mjolner was with me. As sleepy as ever, though. He made a beeline for the bed and curled up on the pillow.

Cats sleep a lot, but this was excessive even for Mjolner. When I was done with Njorun, if I had any energy left, I should really try drawing Mjolner and see if I could see what he was up to.

He opened one eye as if hearing my thoughts and made a low warning sound.

"Are you sure?" I asked him.

He growled again, then closed his eye and went back to sleep.

Whatever he was up to, apparently it was all his business. I would have to respect that. Even though I was growing a bit worried about it.

Njorun climbed into the wagon and sat on the stool, but I perched on the edge of the bunk. From across the table, I could only see her top half, but from the edge of the bunk, I could see her from head to toe.

Not that I knew why that mattered. It was just a gut instinct.

But then my gut reached for the graphite pencils again, and my heart sank. This was going to be Hulda all over again, wasn't it?

Mjolner snuggled deeper into the pillow, a single paw rasping gently against the back of my jeans. He purred, his paw still on me even as he slept.

"Well, nothing to do but try, right?" I said to Njorun.

She didn't reply. But I hadn't honestly expected her to.

I touched my lightest pencil to paper and began to trace the outlines of her form as faintly as I could.

Before I had even finished the first tentative line, I was gone.

I was no longer in a wagon in the middle of a meadow in the wilds of the north. I seemed to be sitting in a sunlit room of a timber-framed house. I was by an open window, the light coming in over my shoulder to fall over the page in front of me. But I wasn't drawing in a book. I was drawing on an old-fashioned easel.

And before me was a girl of about twelve, posing not unlike Hulda had done on the log earlier, head held high and hands clasping one knee as she rocked back ever so slightly, her long, blonde hair hanging loose behind her, its ends sweeping the floorboards.

Her blue eyes looking back at me were clearer than I had ever seen them, but familiar all the same.

Njorun. A young Njorun, dressed in the same gown I had always seen her in, only now it was fresh and new. And she was posing gracefully, waiting for me to finish her portrait.

But just where we were, I had no idea.

CHAPTER EIGHTEEN

THE GIRL POSING before me was sitting at a three-quarters angle from me, her eyes looking out a different window than the one that illuminated my easel. But she glanced my way, then widened her eyes in surprise. She almost dropped her pose, but tensed up again with a swiftness that told me she had been reprimanded to stay still, probably a lot of times.

"You're different," she said.

"Am I?" I said, not sure what she meant. But I was pretty sure who she was. "Njorun?"

"Yes?" she said. She had returned her gaze to a thousand-mile stare out the window, but she chanced another quick look my way.

"Do you know who I am?" I asked her.

She thought about this for a moment, then made the smallest of shrugs. "Not really. Did my parents hire you to take the place of the last fellow?"

"No," I said. Was I in her memory? A memory of a version of Njorun who had never been to the north, never gotten lost in the wilds, never met me or even Reginleif?

But if that were true, why was I here?

I looked at the drawing on the easel before me. It was a mostly finished pencil sketch, not bad, but definitely not my work. No clues there. I set my pencil down, then got up to cross the sunlit room. Njorun shot a few more nervous looks my way but didn't move a muscle, not even when I crouched down in front of her.

"Njorun, are you sure you don't remember me?" I asked her, taking her hands. "Look at me and see if something comes to mind."

Twelve-year-old Njorun turned to face me, squeezing my hands in hers, and looked at me with a grave expression on her young face. She was taking me seriously. That was good.

Then suddenly she sucked in a breath, rocking back on the stool as if she had been struck by an errant wind.

"Njorun?" I said as she flinched away from me, her eyes closed tight.

"I know you," she said, but didn't unclench her body or open her eyes. She had an iron grip on my hands.

"Who am I?" I asked her.

"Ingrid Torfudottir," she said, and finally relaxed her hold on my hands, then relaxed the rest of her body. But she kept her eyes closed, tipping her head down so that the lengths of her blonde hair slid like curtains around her face. "I will know you, one day."

"Will know?" I said.

She nodded miserably. "I've had so many good days. So many. But I never forget for long." She sucked in a shaking breath. "I am a torment to my parents."

"How so?"

"I remember things that haven't happened yet, and no one believes me," she said. "I know I will be cursed, some day. I think that day is coming. Soon I will look like an old crone and will wander a wilderness like nothing I've ever seen."

"Because you're cursed?" I asked, squinting my eyes to try to look at her with my magical senses.

But she shook her head and said impatiently, "not *yet*. Soon, I said. But I remember now things that will happen then. Like you. And

Reginleif. And your grandmother Nora. I always liked... like... liked Nora."

"You remember everything that will happen? Every day of it? Your whole life from now until you're very, very old?" I asked her. That sort of thing had troubled Leifr, who had been taken from Villmark as a small child, then lived out centuries only to return with only a number of decades having passed for the rest of us. And yet he looked like he'd only aged a few years. The compression and dilation of time both, it was hard to wrap your head around. I could only imagine what it was like, living a life like that. But I could never really know.

"I don't grow old," she said sullenly. "I'm going to be cursed, and then I'll be old, all in the blink of an eye."

"Cursed by who? For what reason?" I asked her. Not that I had any idea how I could go about saving her from her fate. But there had to be something I could do.

"I don't know," she sighed. "It's the one thing I know I can't see."

"But you know it's soon," I said.

She nodded.

"I'm not very strong with magic myself, but there might be some things I can try. Something that might protect you," I said. Although I found myself in this sunny room with no wand, no cat, nothing but a pencil.

But sometimes that was enough.

"No, it's no use," Njorun told me. "Reginleif and Nora both tried. Separately and together. No offense, but I don't think you'll succeed where they failed."

"I'm inclined to agree with you," I admitted. "Sorry."

"It's all right," she said, then finally tossed the hair out of her face and looked up at me. "That's not why you're here, anyway. Is it? You need my help."

"I thought I did, but I'm not sure what to ask you as you are now," I said.

"I look like a child, but I'm also the crone you remember," she said, tapping her temple to remind me she had all the memories.

"Do you know what happened to Reginleif, then?" I asked her.

"Some," she said. "You found the poisoned needle blade?"

"I did."

"That's not the murder weapon," she said. "Although it was supposed to be. That's why when you found it, the poison was still there, but there was no blood. Anyone cleaning blood off the blade would've removed the poison as well. But Hulda put it back in Thorfinna's chest without cleaning it at all, and the poison ate into the metal."

"Hulda did it?" I asked. Not that I was at all surprised.

"She took the weapon from the little shadow man, but she didn't use it," Njorun said.

"Maybe you should back up a little," I said.

"Oh, right. Sorry," she said. "There was a little man running through the camp. He showed up after everyone else was asleep. I saw him from where I was sitting by the bonfire, alone. Well, Thorfinna was there, but she was sleeping. Snoring like a bear. You know how she is."

"Sure," I said. "But this man?"

"He was in the shadows. I never got a very good look at him," she said. "But Hulda was awake when he turned up. She was out in the meadow collecting dew into a silver basin under the moonlight. That sort of nonsense," she said and rolled her eyes.

"She says it keeps her beautiful," I said.

"She says," young Njorun agreed with a conspiratorial gleam to her eyes. But then she grew serious again. "The man approached her first, as she was bathing her face. I don't know what he said to her, but she got up and sneaked into Yngvildr's tent to retrieve the poison, then into Thorfinna's wagon to get the blade. She took it across the meadow."

Njorun sighed heavily, then went on. "I knew where she was going. The stones. And I knew why. I could see by the lights in the sky that Reginleif was doing that ritual she does. I don't know what it means, but she does it every year. This year was particularly bright, though. And she had slipped away to do it so very early in the night. It felt like it was important."

"So it wasn't exactly odd that Hulda was heading that way?" I said.

"No, I suppose not," she said. "But I never knew Hulda to have that sort of darkness in her heart. So I got up and followed her, just to see. I doubted I would be able to intervene. I didn't remember then what was going to happen, which meant it was important. The important things are always dark to me. It's maddening."

"I bet," I said with great empathy. It was worse than Cassandra of Troy in a way. To only remember the mundane things that were going to happen. But I supposed that was one way for fate to stay on its course.

"Hulda approached Reginleif as she was coloring the stones with her blood," young Njorun went on, "but then she just stopped. She had the blade in her hand, and it was poised up to strike. But then it was like she just woke up. She snapped awake, saw the blade in her hand, and ran away."

"Back to camp?"

"Not right away," Njorun said. "At first it was like she was trying to hide, or to hide the blade. Only she never stopped anywhere she could've gotten rid of it. Like the pools under the waterfall. She just kept moving, all around the meadow. I think she was still fighting the shadow man's magic."

"Then what happened?" I asked.

"While she was doing that, the shadow man thing appeared outside the circle of light from the stones. Reginleif was still there, still coloring the stones. She had never reacted to Hulda approaching her from behind, but this creature she sensed. She started to get up, to turn to face him, but he was faster."

"But how did he kill her? There were no marks on her body," I said.

"He had a different sort of blade, like he was a different sort of man," she said. She shivered, but forced herself to go on. "I've never seen anything like him, and I have memories for decades before and after that night. Do you understand? He was entirely unique."

"Okay, but different how?" I pressed.

"It was like he wasn't really there," she said. "Not really. It was like he was a shadow or something. The grass didn't move when he passed through it, and no one else saw him but me. Reginleif sensed him, but only too late."

"So he stabbed her with a blade of shadow, and it left no mark," I said.

"And he was so much of shadow, even your magic didn't see him," she said. "I don't know what he is."

"Yeah, me neither," I said.

"But he stabbed her with a knife, and the knife melted into her. Then she started leaking power. I could see it, so bright it hurt to look at. She sort of stumbled back into the grass, and the shadow man took her knife from her. He could touch that, but I don't think the knife liked it, being touched by him. There was an angry flash of light, and I had to cover my eyes until it was gone. When I could see again, the man had disappeared like he had never been there at all, but Reginleif wasn't dead yet."

"She wasn't?"

"No, but she knew it was happening, that it was close. She gathered up all that power she had been leaking, and she put it in the stones."

"And Kara and I drew it out again," I guessed.

"Nilda has some too," young Njorun told me. "Not as much, as she made no offering, but the day before the Dísablót, she had touched the stone with her bare skin. It formed a bond."

"But that was before Reginleif died?" I said.

Young Njorun shrugged. "I'm not the only thing in this world that exists outside of linear time."

"You've talked to someone else about this," I guessed. "Not what happened with Reginleif, what's happening to you."

"Yes, I have," she said. "I remember what he told me. About time and curses. But in the end, he couldn't help me either."

"I'm really sorry about that," I said, but she just shrugged again. "So at some point, Hulda put that blade back. Then lied about it?"

"I don't think so," Njorun said. "I mean, I saw her put it back, but it was like she was walking in her sleep. Her eyes were open, but unseeing. And once she put it back, she went to bed herself. I never once got the sense afterward that she was lying. I think she truly woke up when she chose not to do that shadow man's bidding, but after Reginleif died, he could control her again. She hid the evidence and forgot all of it, just like he wanted her to."

"Do you know where she is now?" I asked.

She gave me a deeply confused look, then glanced around the room as if she, too, had no idea where we were.

"I mean, a day after the murder, she just disappeared. Tent and all. Do you know where?" I asked.

"I don't think I ever saw her again," young Njorun said.

"Is it possible something messed with your memory, like it messed with Hulda's memory?" I asked her.

A single tear slipped down her cheek, but she back-handed it away almost aggressively. "I ask myself that every day. Or every day I can. So many days, it's all I can do to get words out. Once I'm cursed, I can't make what's in my head come out of my mouth. Almost never, anyway."

"You're sure there's no way for me to help you?" I asked.

"I know you try," she said with a weak smile. "I know you fail."

That was probably the most disheartening thing I had ever heard.

"You should probably go," she said with a sniffle. "The real artist is coming back. You can't stay here."

I was going to tell her I had no idea how to get back, but then I blinked my eyes and suddenly I was back in the wagon, looking at old Njorun in the tattered remains of what had once been a very lovely summer gown.

"Njorun?" I said.

But Njorun said nothing, just slid off the stool as if I had dismissed her and hopped out of the wagon.

Was she still twelve, inside of that? And yet the twelve-year-old I had met had been exceedingly mature for her age. And Njorun's child-like air felt like it skewed a lot younger.

Whoever had cursed her, for whatever reason, the curse that held her was a real doozy. But if my grandmother and Reginleif together hadn't been able to help her, I would be draining myself for no reason if I even made an attempt.

Now was not the time. But I was sure I could always go north again and find her. When I had more power, and more time, and a lot more skill. I could find her and try to break her curse.

After all, the breaking of the curse had to be one of those big events that were blocked from her nonlinear memory.

In my bones, I knew it wasn't hopeless.

CHAPTER NINETEEN

Silence hung over all of us gathered around the campfire for a long time after I had finished telling the others what I had seen and heard while drawing Njorun's portrait.

Strangely, I had a finished drawing in my book. Quite a good one. But not a magical one. Visiting her younger self was the magical part, and I had no evidence to offer the others beyond my mere word.

For her part, Njorun was wandering around the meadow again. It took an effort of will to remember she was one of us, to look to see where she was. It no longer felt odd that we had kept forgetting to keep track of her before. It had to be related to her curse somehow.

"We need to make a decision," I told the others. "It's too late to leave now, but in the morning we have to go somewhere. Either we go to find Hulda, in case she does remember something or know something that might be useful, or we go to find the Thors."

"Not the shadow man?" Nilda asked.

"No, that would be fruitless, wouldn't it?" Thorfinna asked, her voice muffled as she talked without taking her chin out of her hands first. She carried on staring glumly into the fire without explaining her remark.

"From what Njorun said, I don't think we'd have much luck

trying to find him," I said. "He doesn't interact with the world. He's invisible to all save her and possibly someone with Reginleif's power. And he's invisible to my magic. It's possible Mjolner can see him, but if that were true, I would think Mjolner would've led us to him already."

"I think he was probably a servant of something else," Kara said. "Don't you get that sense? That he was some sort of magical casting or enthralled spirit or something and not the entity that actually wanted Reginleif eliminated?"

"It's a possibility," I said. "But I don't know how we'd figure any of that out, either. Unless our paths cross again, I don't know how to even start looking for him. Only that, possibly, he might be connected to either Hulda or to whatever is holding the Thors."

"Hence the vote," Nilda said.

"I vote to find Hulda," Yngvildr said. "I'm worried what she might be up to. She fled rather than tell us what she knew—"

"She told all she knew," Thorfinna interrupted to say. "If she had been holding back or lying, Ingrid here would've known."

Everyone looked at me. "Well, I hope that would be true," I offered.

"Still," Yngvildr went on. "She's trouble. And she left without a word. That's not something innocent people do."

"And the fact that she's both easier to find and probably south of here, in the lands you prefer to haunt, is just a happy coincidence?" Thorfinna said in a taunting tone.

Yngvildr's cheeks flushed a deep red. "I meant what I said. Whatever you might think."

"Do you know where she is?" I asked her.

She shook her head sadly. "I have some ideas, but it would take time to travel to them all, and I'm not sure which is the most likely. Plus, I know she stays on the move. It's not as easy as Thorfinna makes it sound."

"Neither option is going to be easy," I said.

"Well, I'm sure this comes as no surprise, but I vote we find the Thors," Thorfinna said, finally sitting up on her stool and slapping her hands on her thighs. "I think the odds are good that what was done to

Reginleif was done to stop her from protecting them. This is all about them. We'll find our answers when we find them."

"But we don't know where to start there either, do we?" Nilda said.

"Like Yngvildr, I have some ideas," Thorfinna said. "Some good ones. Plus, they are a damn sight closer to us than the places Hulda likely ran to."

"You haven't asked the *spiders*."

We all jumped at that voice suddenly speaking among us. But it was only Njorun, back from her wanderings.

Only she was clearly speaking in great earnest. Her bony hands were balled into fists and her entire posture was like someone trying to lift a heavy burden. All just to get those words out.

"What did you say?" Kara asked her.

But when Njorun opened her mouth again, all that came out was that same strange variant of Norse, and in a babbling rush at that.

And yet her younger self had spoken perfect Villmarker Norse. Was that part of the magic that took me there that let me understand her, or was this language she spoke now part of the curse?

"She said something about spiders before," Nilda pointed out.

"And that drawing with the Thors in it, it looked like they were caught in webs," Kara added.

"And Hulda too," Yngvildr put in.

"It's all connected," I said. "Maybe it doesn't matter in the end which way we go first."

No one said anything. But it felt to me like they were all holding their breath, watching me think and waiting for me to speak. Just by necessity, I turned my back on the fire and walked away, taking as many steps as I needed for that feeling of expectation smothering me to fade just a little.

So many prejudices were muddling my thoughts now, I didn't think it was going to be possible for me to make a clear-headed, logical decision.

Despite Njorun's insistence that Hulda had broken free from the spell that had compelled her to murder Reginleif, I still didn't trust her. There were too many overlaps between how she was and how

Halldis had been when I first met her. I knew even if murder was beyond her, lesser troublemaking was not.

I didn't think she would kill anyone herself. But I totally believed she would lure others to their deaths. And the shadow man, whoever he was, had surely picked her to be his proxy for some other reason than that she happened to be awake at the time.

Still, Thorfinna wasn't wrong. She was probably long gone from here, and we'd likely have to chase her for days and days. In the exact opposite direction to the one I really wanted to be going.

But that was the other prejudice clouding my decision-making abilities. There was nowhere I wanted to be more, and nothing I wanted to be doing more desperately, than finding the Thors.

And I had believed Thorfinna when she said she knew they were close. Certainly closer than Hulda.

The only thing my gut was telling me was finding one would lead to the other. Because they were caught in the same web. My gut was very clear on that score. And I was pretty sure it was seeing with clearer eyes than my mind.

I turned and walked back to the fire, feeling that expectation thick in the air, growing thicker with every step. It made my throat feel like it wanted to close up. I wasn't worthy of all these people looking to me for guidance. I didn't know any better than they did.

And yet, I was in charge because I had *taken* charge. So it was my responsibility now.

"Listen," I said as I reached the fire, but for once I actually noticed that Njorun wasn't there. "Where's Njorun?" I asked.

"Does she have to be here for this?" Thorfinna asked, sounding genuinely confused.

"I think she went in your wagon, actually," Kara said, almost guiltily.

"Njorun!" I called. The door at the back of the wagon stood open, but the interior was in shadows. And nothing moved within.

I walked over and poked my head inside. Mjolner was just sitting up on the bunk to blink at me sleepily, but he was the only living thing inside.

And yet, I could tell Njorun had been there just a moment before. The smell of her lingered in the air, for one.

For the other, my grandmother's map was left out on the little table. I pushed the forks and spoons that had been weighing down the edges away, then carried it back to the fire.

"What's that? Your grandmother's map?" Kara asked, and she and Nilda both got up to look at it as I spread it wide, angled to catch the best light from the fire. The sun had dipped below the hills to the west and while the sky was still pink near the horizon, the light was too dim to read by.

"Njorun made some additions," I said, leaning in close to examine the drawing. "I do believe she's told us where the Thors are."

Thorfinna got up so suddenly she sent her stool tumbling to the ground behind her. I let her have the map at once, worried it would tear if I tried to keep a hold of it. She unrolled it between her own hands and examined it, then grunted appreciatively.

"Yes, just where I was thinking of going," she said. Then flushed pinkly as she added, "but not the first place. This does save us some time."

"I assumed I was outvoted," Yngvildr said. " The three of you never said, but I guess you didn't have to."

"Actually, that's what I was just going to ask you about," I said. "There's no reason for us all to stay together, and every reason to split up and pursue both directions."

"You want me to go after Hulda?" Yngvildr asked, then looked around at the others. "Alone?"

"I'll go with you," Nilda said, touching her hand to the hilt of her sword. "Is that what you were going to suggest, Ingrid?"

It hadn't been, but it made so much more sense than sending Yngvildr on her own after a potentially dangerous target. "If you're sure?"

"Thorfinna is more than able to take my place," Nilda said with the faintest hint of a smile in her eyes. "And I think Yngvildr won't mind my company too much."

"No, certainly not!" Yngvildr said with a wide grin. "It would be appreciated. So very much."

"We'll meet up again after you've found the Thors," Nilda said. "If not in Villmark, I'm sure you can find us."

"Here," I said, taking the spear pendant from around my neck and putting it around Nilda's.

"But this is your grandmother's!" she objected.

"And as such, I will always be able to find it again," I told her. "As long as you keep it with you, I'll be able to find you."

"You're sure?" she asked me.

"It suits you," Kara said, even as I nodded.

"It does," I said. "I know my grandmother won't mind. She's about to have a whole wagon full of things to remember Reginleif by."

"Then at first light of dawn, we part ways," Thorfinna said. She was bouncing on the balls of her feet, and I knew if I had said the word, she would've started our journey at that very moment. No matter how risky it would be to take the wagons down unknown roads in the dark.

"But what about Njorun?" Kara asked. "Is she going with us or with Yngvildr and Nilda?"

"Njorun has already gone," I said, certain it was true. I could sense she was no longer in the meadow between the waterfalls. She had told me all I needed to know, and then she had moved on to wherever she had to be next.

"She's helped enough, if this map is true," Thorfinna said.

CHAPTER TWENTY

WHAT NJORUN HAD ADDED to my grandmother's map was a single tower, almost featureless, tucked among the mountains. My grandmother had added few details to this part of the map, just the slopes of the mountains themselves. There were no clues as to who might dwell there, or what monsters we might encounter.

It was deceptive. It looked like a straight shot. It looked like we'd be there in just a few days of hard hiking.

But the first thing Thorfinna did after we had loaded up the wagons—and said farewell to Yngvildr and Nilda, who were on foot for their journey south—was to tell me to put the map away and not take it out again.

"This is the north," she had told me and Kara. "It has its own rules."

I didn't get the rules at all. To me, it felt like we were just wandering about, choosing directions when the road forked by random.

Wasting time.

It was disheartening. Maddening, really. With every passing hour, my urgency grew, and yet it seemed as if we made no progress.

"You need to want it less," Thorfinna told me when we had stopped for the fourth night without drawing any closer to those mountains, let alone finding that tower.

"I don't think that's possible," I said.

"You're a volva. Anything is possible," Thorfinna scoffed.

I looked at Kara, but Kara just shrugged. "Maybe she's right?"

"Even if she is, I don't know how to start not caring," I said helplessly.

"I have an idea," Kara said, but refused to say more until the next morning, the morning of the fifth day. After a quick breakfast, Thorfinna climbed onto her wagon to get her horse going, but Kara took my place driving the ox.

"You wanted to drive? That was your idea?" I said. I doubted very much that Kara wanted to find the Thors less than I did.

"I think this will work, not because I'm driving, but because since you have so much more power than I, if you're distracted, it might be enough," she said.

"I don't get you," I admitted.

But she held out my art bag. "I want you to ride beside me, but don't think about where we're going. Just draw where we are. Really think about where we are."

"Right," I said, not as kindly as Kara deserved, but the best I could do. I was feeling more than a little surly, and secretly sure this wasn't going to work.

But I owed it to her to at least try.

So I drew the forest around us, the meadows we crossed, the clouds in the sky. And always, inevitably, the mountains on the horizon, never drawing nearer.

But then the reidh rune started sneaking into the pictures. Subtly at first, but then more forcefully. Strangely, as much as I understood that rune to be about taking a journey, what it kept calling to mind was my home back in Villmark.

This journey was just a big circle, in the end. Out into the north, but then back home again. To where my people were waiting. For the Thors, true, but for me too. I knew it.

I turned page after page in my sketchbook, adding drawing after drawing. I had only barely noticed how it was getting harder to see the paper when the wagons slowed, and I realized we were stopping for the night.

And we were there, in the proper foothills of the mountains. I could smell the snowmelt on the air from the high peaks that towered right above us. I could hear raptors calling as they hunted, spiraling high over our heads in that last light of day.

"It worked!" I said.

"We're close, but we're not there yet," Thorfinna said. "Keep it up tomorrow and then we'll see."

I knew she was right, but I couldn't tamp down the excitement in my belly. I knew we were close. I could feel Thorbjorn somewhere just out of reach.

I could also feel that he was in no way aware of me, but that was okay. I'd be face to face with him soon enough.

The next morning, we followed the same plan, but it felt to me like it derailed almost at once. I couldn't focus on the world around me like I was supposed to. I just kept drawing the same tower over and over again. It wasn't exactly like Njorun's tower. And every iteration was slightly different from the ones before. It was like I was trying to picture it in my mind and draw it on the paper, but that something kept interfering in that process over and over again.

Then it started to rain, and I had to put my book and pencils away. Short of going inside the wagon, there was no way to keep drawing with the fat drops of water soaking the paper. The tip of the pencil just tore the page without leaving a mark.

But after putting the book away, I finally looked around at where we were. After drawing that tower for hours, I was startled to find we had climbed quite a lot in elevation. I could see the edge of the snowfield so close I could run to it if I hopped off the wagon.

"Don't look now," Kara whispered to me, "but is that it?"

There was no way to obey her command *and* answer her question. I opted to glance up only briefly, my head tipped down so I could see my own brow line blocking most of my view.

But not all of it. One quick look was all I needed. She was right. I could see the top of the tower ahead of us, almost obscured by the clouds that were descending all around us as the rain pounded on.

"One more turn of this road should do it," Kara said, and urged the ox to pick up the pace. But the ox ignored her, plodding on as steadily as ever.

Thorfinna, in her wagon behind us, was singing. The patter of the rain obscured most of her words, but her rumbling voice carried in a driving beat. It syncopated with the ox's hooves on the rocky ground of the mountain road. It was a repetitive song, and each time the refrain came around again, Thorfinna bellowed it all the louder.

Just when I thought I could make out some of the words, a sudden rumble of thunder drowned them out again. The rumble didn't fade like thunder usually did, though. It built, louder and louder, until it ended with a crack.

And a bolt of lightning stabbed down out of the sky to strike a rocky prominence just above the road.

"Run!" Kara yelled. At first I thought she was talking to me, but as she whipped at the reins, I realized it was the ox she was talking to. And for once the ox responded, leaning into the yoke to propel the wagon through the narrow pass in the rocks. I could hear rocks tumbling down, but I was still momentarily blinded from looking straight at that bolt of lightning.

Once we were clear of the pass, Kara pulled the ox to a halt, then spun in her seat to look back. The tumble of rocks was louder than the thunder now, and I didn't see how Thorfinna could possibly make it in time.

The first few rocks struck the road, sinking into the muddy ground in deep craters and tearing up the rocky surface in plates around it.

Then I heard Thorfinna shout—a high, wild sound—and her horse leaped well over those knee-high boulders, pulling the wagon in an arc after it, Thorfinna and all.

That was some impressive horse.

The wagon landed on the far side with a wheel-crunching crash into the ground. But that sound was muted against the backdrop of falling rock that filled the pass behind us.

"I guess we're not going back that way!" Thorfinna said with a crazy grin.

"Good thing we're there then," Kara said mildly, pointing through the thickening rain to the base of the tower.

It was close, very close. It would only take a minute or two to run to it.

If not for the chasm between the road and it.

"What do we do now?" I asked.

"This part I can handle," Thorfinna said, and jumped down from the seat of her wagon. She gave her horse an appreciative pat before going to the back of her wagon and digging around inside.

She came back with a length of rope attached to an arrow. Just like I had seen in countless movies.

And always rolled my eyes at the fakery of Hollywood. That rope was too heavy for that arrow, I just knew it.

There was no way this was going to work.

She walked up to the edge to line up her shot using the tallest longbow I had ever seen. That, plus her bulging arms, made me reconsider my opinion a little bit. I adjusted it to "if anyone can do it, she can."

Kara hopped down from the wagon and led the ox to a narrow meadow on the far side of the road from the chasm. She opened the chest under the driver's seat and took out the tarp to make his tent and a small trough for his food. I hopped down too, making myself useful by filling the trough with feed from the sack, also under the seat, then filling a pail with water to set under the tent Kara had hastily erected over him.

He deserved better, but even if that tower had a stable, there was no way we were going to get him over to it.

"Sorry, buddy," I said to him. He blew out a breath that clouded in the cold air, then put his face into the feed trough. Then Kara and I went to do the same with Thorfinna's horse.

By the time we were finished, Thorfinna had two ropes suspended across the chasm. The ones on our side were firmly anchored into the rock face with long iron nails.

But the ones on the other side were still attached to the arrows. The arrows were embedded in a very dead-looking tree, and that tree was already half tumbled over into the chasm itself.

"I don't think this is going to work," I said.

"Nonsense!" Thorfinna said, tugging on the ropes to demonstrate how solid they were.

I was sure I saw one of the arrows start to pull free. But it stopped again, seemingly fast once more.

Another bolt of lightning hit the rock behind us, sending another avalanche into that mountain pass.

"We should get inside," Kara said. Then she grabbed onto the ropes. With her feet on one and her hands on the other, she slide-stepped across the chasm to the far side. She wrapped her arms around the tree, then clambered around it to push herself upright on the far side.

"You next," Thorfinna told me.

That was logical. Thorfinna weighed a lot more than I did. But looking down into that chasm, logic was pretty far from my mind.

But then I saw Kara on the other side, waving excitedly for me to hurry and follow.

She had seen them. She had seen the Thors.

That was all the motivation I needed. I clung to that rope in an iron grip, and I shuffled my feet much more slowly than Kara had, but I made it across. And, unlike Kara, I had someone waiting for me on the other side to give me a hand up onto the ledge of ground around the base of the tower.

Thorfinna followed far more nimbly than I would've thought.

"You saw them?" I said to Kara as we waited for Thorfinna to reach our side.

"They're all in there," she said. "But they didn't wake up when I opened the door. I guess because of the storm, maybe they didn't hear me?"

"They'll hear Thorfinna for sure," I said, and we exchanged a smile.

Then Thorfinna was pulling herself around the tree, and the three of us wasted no time getting to the door. The rain was turning to snow, and I spared a brief moment worrying about our animals camping on the side of the road.

Then we were inside the tower, and before I had even had time to let my eyes adjust to the darkness, I heard the unmistakable sound of Mjolner meowing at me in a "what took you so long?" tone.

He was indeed there, just outside of the reach of the snow that had blown in with us. Then Thorfinna closed the heavy door behind us, and the storm was nothing more than a low howl of noise, easily tuned out.

I looked around the interior of the tower. It was all one space, from floor to ceiling far overhead. If there had ever been a staircase up the interior to the lookout on top, it was long gone now. We were standing in a completely unadorned cylinder of gray stone. As much as a round space can have corners, this place had suggestions of them where heavy, dust-laden cobwebs hung particularly thickly.

There was no fireplace or chimney, just a massive fire pit in the center of the tower that reminded me of the ancestral fire back in Villmark. It crackled with flames, although given that no one was tending the fire, I would've expected it to be burned down to embers.

Only gradually did I realize the lumps in the shadows close to the walls of the tower were beds. They were set as far from the fire with its light and warmth as possible. There were six beds, equally distant from each other around the tower floor. And each bed had a single occupant.

Without a word to each other, we each walked up to a different bed.

"Thoralv," I said, recognizing the youngest of the Thors by his spiky hair. Normally he was the only brother with no beard, but he had a considerable amount of reddish-gold whiskers on his jaw now.

"Frór," Thorfinna said. I could just see the top of his dark head over the edge of the ratty old fur that covered him and guessed she was right.

"Thorge," Kara said, her voice thick with emotion. She had pulled back the covers, and I could see the back of his ginger head. I had to take her at her word that it was Thorge, as the sides of his head which he usually kept closely shaved were now so overgrown I could no longer make out the knotwork tattoos he had curved over each ear.

I moved to the next bed and saw Thormund, the second oldest of the brothers. His long hair and beard were still in their braids, but many strands had worked their way loose.

The next bed contained Thorulv, the oldest. His long beard was tucked under his folded arms, and his shaved head also had grown in, although there was some silver in that reddish-gold I hadn't expected to see.

"Ingrid," Kara said, and I ran to where she was at the sixth bed.

It was Thorbjorn. I had finally found him.

Thorfinna had said they had been moving like they were sleep-walking when she had seen them last. But that was no longer true. They didn't look like they'd been walking in quite some time.

They had been in these beds for so long, cobwebs were draped all over them. And nothing Kara, Thorfinna, and I could do would wake them. We shook them, shouted at them, even tried to roll them out of the beds.

But we couldn't get their eyes to open. And not even Thorfinna could spill them out of those beds.

This was definitely magic. Only I still couldn't sense it.

CHAPTER TWENTY-ONE

THE RAIN that had been turning to snow when we'd been outside was a full-blown blizzard now. Blasts of wind whistled and howled around the stone walls of the tower around us. I could almost see those walls shifting in that wind. I remembered how narrow the strip of rock had been that had extended beyond the tower walls. How very long the drop was to the bottom of the chasm all around us.

I was still sitting on the edge of Thorbjorn's bed. I had his hand in mine. I could feel his pulse, but only when I searched for it. It was weak and slow, and his flesh was so very cold.

And yet the fire in the center of the room blazed so warmly I was sweating.

"Ingrid, what's that smell?" Kara asked me from where she was sitting on Thorge's bed.

At first, I wasn't sure what she meant. Dust and cobweb smell was the strongest by far, and under that was a mustiness that came from the very old bedding. Not that the Thors were smelling so great themselves. Shaving wasn't the only bit of hygiene they were behind on.

But then I got a whiff of something else, and I realized what had Kara so worried. It was a strange smell, something like burning green wood, but not exactly. I was pretty sure it was the culprit for the headache growing behind my eyes.

"It's coming from that fire," Kara said, and started kicking the logs off the fire, spreading them around the room. I yelped in alarm at the sight of her almost setting herself on fire.

Then Thorfinna threw open the door and let the blizzard rush in. It spun like a snow cyclone in the center of the room, and I got up to join Kara and Thorfinna in stomping the scattered fire out.

When we were done, it was very dark and very cold, but the air was so much fresher I don't think any of us minded.

But none of the Thors stirred. Snow settled on their upturned faces and folded hands, but they slept on, undisturbed.

"Now what?" Thorfinna asked, panting from the effort of stomping out the fire.

"Now we clean," I said, pointing up to the cobwebs that hung all around us.

We had no tools for this job, but the musty sheets that lurked under the bear hides on the Thors' beds served as rags well enough. Thorfinna could reach higher than the rest of us, and she spun a single sheet into a whip to further extend her reach.

And Kara proved herself to be a very accomplished scaler of walls. I thought I had been nervous when she'd charged into the fire, but that was nothing compared to watching as she climbed around and around the interior of the tower, sending dust-choked cobwebs raining down on us.

When she safely came down again, we brushed off the Thors, then used the hides to sweep everything towards the door. Thorfinna opened that door again, and we threw everything over the side, into the chasm below.

Then she went around the outside curve of the tower until she found the twisted remains of another tree, like the one we had our rope bridge attached to. She strained to uproot the stubborn tree, then dragged the entire thing into the tower.

It certainly smelled better inside the tower, and our heads felt clearer than before. Soon Thorfinna had broken the tree down and used it to build a less tainted fire. It didn't light up the space as brightly as the other fire had done, but it did warm up the space around it.

Kara and I worked together to pull the beds closer to that fire. We had taken their sheets and bear hides, but we couldn't get them off the beds or get the moldy mattresses out from underneath them.

"I thought for sure the fire was enchanting them," Kara said.

"I did too," I said. "Maybe it takes longer for the effects to wear off on them? Who knows how long they were breathing it?"

"It's magic," Thorfinna said as she poked at the fire. "Isn't there anything you can do against this magic?"

"I don't even *see* this magic," I said, but I took out my bronze wand. I waved it in front of my eyes and examined everything in that tower, especially the Thors and their beds. Mjolner followed me around with great interest.

But I still could see nothing.

I put the wand away and sat with the others around the little fire.

"Maybe when the storm stops, we can try bringing them outside," Kara said. "Fresh air might help."

"There's no way we're getting them back to the road," I said. "I don't think even Thorfinna could make that climb with a Thor on her back, let alone all five of them, plus Frór."

"I would be willing to try," Thorfinna said stoutly.

"I'm going to try drawing this space," I said, taking my sketchbook out of my bag.

"You didn't see that shadow man before," Kara said worriedly. "If he's the one doing this, or it's part of the same magic that created him, what good will drawing do?"

"More good than doing nothing," Thorfinna chided her.

I gave Kara a chagrined shrug. "It can't hurt to try."

Although that wasn't exactly true. Drawing while in a fugue state left me vulnerable to others' magic. If the shadow man was really here with us in the tower, like the little voice in the back of my mind kept whispering to me, I could be putting myself in real danger.

But I looked over at Thorbjorn sleeping on despite the blue hue to his skin from the persistent cold. I had to try.

I put charcoal to paper and started sketching. But I didn't start with drawing the Thors and the beds. I started by looking straight up towards the top of the tower, lost in shadow high above us. I drew that, a perspective drawing from inside a cylinder. The artist part of my brain was pretty geeked about that challenge.

That geeking out was the last thing I remembered. Then I was gone.

Until a splash of frigid water struck me full in the face. I woke sputtering and, I'll admit it, swearing a bit.

"Sorry," Kara said, standing over me with a now empty bucket. "There was no other way."

I touched my cheek and felt the prickle from the ghost of a slap I had slept through. But this one felt like a real doozy. I looked from Kara to Thorfinna, who flushed red.

"Sorry," she said. "You're going to have a bruise."

"But we had to bring you out," Kara said, pointing to the beds around us. "You were making it worse."

I looked around and saw all the Thors and Frór thrashing on their mattresses. They weren't awake, not remotely. But they were clearly having night terrors of the first order. Some were crying out, others almost sobbing.

"We tried water on them, too, but it did nothing," Kara said. "What did you see?"

"I don't know," I admitted, then looked down at the drenched pages of my sketchbook.

"We *did* try slapping first," Thorfinna said.

"It'll dry in a minute," I said with I hope more optimism than I felt. I moved closer to the fire and held the book open, the pages as far apart as I could make them.

The paper, of course, didn't dry as flat as it once was. The whole book was now twice as thick and very bulky. A lot of the charcoal had run as well, and I was covered in black mud made from its dust.

But the drawings were still legible.

I had drawn the inside of the tower like inside the long tube of a telescope many times. It always felt like something lurked in the shadows, but squint and turn the page as I might, I couldn't bring anything into focus.

I kept turning the pages until I got to a sketch that had the Thors in it. But not just the Thors. They were lying sprawled out on those nasty beds, but something was sitting on their chests. Six separate creatures pinning them down and bending over them. Like vampires about to dine.

"What are those?" I asked, not able to discern any features from the water-logged charcoal.

"Maras," Kara told me.

"You mean like nightmares?" I asked. "They look almost like spiders."

"Hag-like creatures that ride the bodies of sleepers," she said, nodding. "No wonder we can't wake them."

"But why can't I see them?" I wondered.

"You did see them," Kara said. "And now we know they're there. That's something."

"But this doesn't make any sense," Thorfinna said. We all looked up at her questioningly, and she went on. "Maras are solitary creatures. We wanderers in the north are particularly prone to them. They plague us easily since we sleep alone, no one to help us wake from their visions."

"So we can wake them?" I asked.

"No, you're missing my point," Thorfinna said. "This isn't right. It isn't natural. Six at once, feeding so vociferously? They don't behave like this. Ever. Something else is going on here."

I looked back down at my drawing, then sighed. "I think I know what you're all going to say, but does it look to you like they are caught in webbing?"

They passed the book between them, but both of them, after examining the drawing, gave me a solemn nod.

"So they're prisoners?" Kara said, looking around as she hugged herself. "What could hold them prisoner?"

"The same thing that sent the shadow man," I said. "This is all connected."

"But what can we do?" Kara asked me imploringly.

I half-closed my eyes, feeling the world around me. I thought I could just sense the Maras, but I might've been projecting because I knew they were there.

But maybe not. Would I project that feeling of being trapped on them? Because I felt it. They were prisoners too; I knew it.

How grateful would they be if I set them free? Would they linger long enough to tell me who had done this to them, and why?

Then I felt something else. Sort of. It was more like I was suddenly aware that there was a corner at the top of the tower that my awareness just kept skipping past.

It reminded me of something we had done in science class when I was a kid, looking at a small image on a page and moving it around until it seemed to disappear when it was in your blind spot. And we had learned how our brains compensate for that blind spot by just filling in the blanks, so our mind's eye saw a continuous background.

That corner of the tower was my magical blind spot, and my magical mind kept trying to fill in what it assumed was there to make a complete background. But now that I knew it was there, I could sense how I didn't really know what was up there.

Unfortunately, knowing that didn't help me see it. It was still a blind spot.

But something was up there, and whatever that thing was, it was working very hard to make sure I didn't notice it lurking.

For all I knew, it was aware that I was now aware, but just in case it didn't know, I opted not to say anything out loud to the others.

"Ingrid?" Kara said.

"Sorry," I said, pressing a hand to my forehead. I was so very tired. But this was no time for sleeping. Not for me, anyway.

Or was it?

"I have an idea," I said. "I think I know how to get the Thors back."

If I had thought the others would tell me I was crazy, I was wrong. Because as soon as I told them what I was thinking, they were all grinning the same foolhardy "let's go for it" grin that I hadn't even realized I had been missing for so many months.

It was the same grin the Thors had before they charged in to fight trolls or giants. Somehow, it felt completely appropriate to dive into rescuing them with that same manic energy.

And with that thought, I was grinning too.

CHAPTER TWENTY-TWO

I FOUND myself wishing we had kept Nilda with us on this leg of the journey. At this point, Nilda knew without asking that her job was going to be watching out for Kara and me. She was used to it. But Thorfinna took a little more convincing.

"Do you have any magical talent at all?" I asked her.

"No, but—" she started to stubbornly say.

But I interrupted her. "And do you have a particularly close bond with any of these men?"

"I have a close bond with all of these men," she insisted, arms crossed as she towered over me.

But I wasn't intimidated. "A two-way bond?"

She scowled at me fiercely.

"It's possible that whatever caused this is going to react to what Kara and I are about to do," I told her. "That's why it's so important that you are ready."

"I can't actually fight magic," Thorfinna said, sounding almost ashamed.

"I have a feeling this is the reason Mjolner has been sleeping so much the last few days," I said. "Or haven't any of you noticed he hasn't napped once since we came inside the tower?"

"He's hunting," Thorfinna said with a shrug. Which was also true. He had been listening to things inside the walls or under the floor and occasionally staring fixedly at something the rest of us couldn't perceive. Classic cat hunting behavior.

But he was fully alert. And currently sitting on Frór's chest. Frór had calmed measurably since Mjolner had hopped up there. But he hadn't woken up.

Whatever Mjolner's magic was—and I'll be the first to admit I don't exactly understand it—it was more defensive than offensive. He would keep me safe from anything, but rescuing others had to be my action, not his.

"I think we should do this quickly," Kara said. "Thorge has been getting paler just since we arrived. Whatever life force that Mara is draining from him, he's almost run dry."

I looked down at Thorbjorn and realized he, too, looked far worse than he had before. His cheeks were downright hollow, and he had dark blue smudges under his fluttering but still closed eyes.

"Thorfinna, help me move the beds closer together," I said, gesturing towards Thorge's and Thorbjorn's beds. "We need to keep in contact, each of us with our Thor, but also with each other."

"I'll push them together," Thorfinna said, and did so.

The bunks were so narrow they barely had room enough for the Thors, but Kara and I somehow squeezed in between Thorge and Thorbjorn.

"What if I can't fall asleep?" Kara whispered to me as Thorfinna turned her attention to building up the fire.

"You will," I assured her. "Just focus on your breathing and your hand in mine."

I put out my hand, and she clasped it. Then we let them drop between us.

As confident as I had tried to sound, I had shared Kara's fear. But in truth, it was far past midnight, after a very full day. Sleep was harder to avoid than to find. It only took a few deep breaths, and I was out like a light.

I found myself standing in the commons in the heart of Villmark, just beside the old well. I could see my house from there.

It was on fire. All of Villmark was on fire. And bodies littered the streets. But these weren't victims of fire or smoke inhalation. They had been chopped, stabbed and bashed by the weapons of some invading force.

The heat from fires all around me was intense, so intense I could feel my skin blistering. The sound of it was a monstrous roar punctuated by timbers cracking like gunshots and then the collapse of a roof or wall. The blowing wind was no relief, only a source of more dense smoke that choked my lungs. But even through the billows of smoke I could smell the coppery scent of blood, the blood that ran through the cobblestones like red rain.

I was in Thorbjorn's nightmare.

I spun around, hoping to find a clue as to where to start looking for him. But then I saw him there, right at my feet. He had collapsed to his knees, half-draped over the stone wall around the well. He was bleeding from more cuts than I could count. An axe and a sword lay on the cobblestones beside him, both broken beyond repair.

And he was weeping.

But even through the smoke and fire, I could sense monsters closing in on us from all sides. They were creeping ever closer, rolling in with a protective fog that clouded my magical sight. But I knew they were there.

"Thorbjorn," I said, putting a hand on his shoulder.

He flinched away from me, striking my hand away in a stinging blow. Then he took up the handle of his broken sword. It was less than a knife, now, but the edges were still sharp.

I had no idea what would happen to me back in the tower if Thorbjorn stabbed me here. What would Thorfinna see? Could she pull me out in time to save me?

I took a few stumbling steps back, raising my hands to show they were empty. "Thorbjorn, it's me. Ingrid."

"Liar!" he bellowed, and lunged to his feet, swinging the broken sword towards my belly. It sliced through the front of my shirt, not quite grazing my skin as I stumbled back again.

I was all too aware of how close those monsters were behind me, but I didn't dare take my eyes off Thorbjorn.

"How can I prove it to you?" I asked. "I still don't remember everything about our childhood together."

"Hush, beast!" he yelled, and charged me with a series of attacks I just barely dodged. I could tell he was tired, but somehow I didn't think he would collapse from exhaustion faster than I was going to mess up dodging out of his way. He was going to cut me if I didn't figure out a way to stop him.

"Thorbjorn," I said again. "It's me, Ingrid. Ingrid Torfudottir. We met on the highway that runs over Runde. I almost hit you with my car. I *did* hit that tree. Don't you remember?"

"You're not her," he growled at me. But there was just a little uncertainty in his eyes. And, I thought, just a little hope as well.

His next swing at me was very sloppy, almost half-hearted, and I easily ducked out of the way.

But then I lunged at him, throwing my arms around his shoulders and hugging him tight. He could throw me off with a simple shake of his shoulders, but he stood there as if frozen.

"I swear it's me, Thorbjorn," I said, as close to his ear as I could reach. "I'm sorry it took so long. You weren't easy to find."

"Ingrid?" he said. I could tell he didn't want to believe it. But he was starting to.

"Yes," I said. He turned around, breaking my hold on him with ridiculous ease. But then he staggered and fell, mostly to his knees but partly on top of me. I couldn't support that kind of weight, especially with no warning. I went down with him, down to the blood-stained cobblestones that were starting to crack from the heat of the fires around us.

"It's you," he said, gripping my arms far too tightly.

I wondered if, back in the tower, Thorfinna could see bruises blossoming on my arms from his fingers.

But I didn't pull away. Not even when he drove his head into my chest with so much force, it knocked the wind out of me. But he was only burying his face against me. I could feel his tears soaking through my shirt.

"It's me," I said, hugging him tightly. "But we have to get out of here."

"We can't win this, Ingrid," he said, his voice muffled against my shirt. "Not even together. We can't win."

"Nonsense," I said. "This is a world of dreams, right? It's been your nightmare for I have no idea how long, but I'm here now. And that Mara isn't feeding on me. She's not in control of me. I have power here she can't touch."

"What do you mean?" he asked, looking up at me.

"I mean, watch," I said, waving a hand over his broken sword and then over his broken axe. That was all it took. His weapons were whole again, gleaming brightly, as if newly forged.

"But it's just an illusion," he said, even as he admired the sword in his hand.

"So is that giant," I said as the first of the monsters emerged from the fog behind him.

Thorbjorn didn't even hesitate. He spun, lunging to his feet and stabbing with his sword all in one smooth motion. And that blade sunk deep into the giant's belly.

The giant fell to the ground and Thorbjorn looked back at me with that manic grin I knew so well. I tossed him his axe, and he saluted me with it then charged at the trio of trolls who were the next out of the fog.

I watched him spin and fight, hearing his battle-cry over and over again.

Then I saw he was no longer alone. Thorge was beside him, his knives in his hands. They fell into a rhythm around each other without so much as a passing glance between them.

These monsters stood no chance.

Kara stepped up beside me, and her hand was in mine. On some level, it had never left. The sensations of this place were starting to blend with the world we had left behind in the tower. I could almost feel that cold, although the sensations of the burning buildings around us were still stronger.

"We have to wake them up now," Kara said.

"The others…" I started to say, but then a blast of wind blew some of the fog and smoke away, and I realized all five brothers were in there now, all fighting together.

And Frór. Who had Mjolner riding his shoulders even as he spun and fought with a giant.

Mjolner saw me and winked a single green eye at me. Cheeky little cat. While Kara and I had freed one Thor each, he had freed all the others plus Frór.

"We've broken them all free," I said. "And yet they're all still fighting. How many monsters are planning on coming out of that smoke and fog?"

"Something must be sending them," Kara said grimly. Then she glanced at me. "Don't you think?"

"I do," I said. I closed my eyes and focused my magical attention on the very heart of that dark place.

It should've been an automatic thing for me now. I'd trained enough in magic that basic awareness came easily to me.

But I wasn't in the physical world. I was in a shared dream world. That changed things. And there were eight of us in there, all dreaming. Mostly together, but there were random bits that one or another of us were generating apart from the others.

All of that plus more was swirling together in the heart of that darkness. I sensed the Maras in there, too. Trapped. They were no longer riding the Thors and Frór, but they were no longer free, either.

I opened the eyes of my dream self then, still holding tight to Kara's hand, I charged into that fog. It only took Kara a fraction of a second to start running, too.

Despite the darkness from the thick billows of smoke, the heat was intense. And I could feel my boots sticking to the blood that was no longer flowing down the streets. It was baking into a congealed mass that clung to the soles of my boots.

"What are we looking for?" Kara asked, wrapping her free arm around her head to protect her eyes from the furnace-like heat.

"He has to be here," I said. Then, on impulse, I just thrust out my free hand.

It closed around something that wanted to disintegrate at my touch. To become no more than smoke itself. But I didn't let it. I made it keep its form. It was like I was channeling the power of the Ur rune.

It worked. I could feel a solid thing inside my grasp. I dragged it out of the smoke, but it was a confusing image. I had something that felt like a man but looked like pure black, billowing smoke.

"The shadow man," Kara said.

The thing stopped struggling against me and turned its attention to her. It had eyes of a sort, like dark embers glowing in a red so dark it was nearly black. I could feel the hate radiating out of him, like the heat around us all.

Then I saw the knife. It hovered in the smoke at about the level it would be if it were clipped to his belt. I let him go, then quickly snatched it away from him, before he had quite escaped.

With a shriek of furious rage, he dissipated, fading into the smoke all around us.

"What is that?" Kara asked.

I showed it to her. "Reginleif's knife, isn't it?" I said.

"He took it from her when he killed her," Kara said. Then she looked up at me. "But why?"

"I think if I draw it, I might figure it out," I said. "But right now, it's time to go."

We emerged from the smoke to find the Thors catching their breath, weapons hanging at their sides. But their eyes were still sweeping all around them, looking for more foes.

"The Maras have gone," I said, and Kara nodded. She felt it too. They were no longer in the dream world with us. "It was the shadow man that was holding them, I guess."

"It looks that way," Kara said. Then she gestured to the Thors. "Do we need to hold on to them to bring them out?"

"I don't think so. They aren't in the thrall of the Maras anymore. They'll wake up on their own," I said.

"Then let's wake up," Kara said.

We both opened our eyes at once, then sat up.

The Thors around us were still sleeping, but it was a deep, natural sleep now. The Maras were gone, but they were still exhausted.

"They'll wake when they're ready," I said.

"I know," Kara said, and pulled me into a tight hug. "We did it."

"We did," I agreed.

But then I felt something shift far above us. Whatever had been lurking in my blind spot was unfolding itself, expanding, descending.

It was coming for me.

CHAPTER TWENTY-THREE

I wanted to look up, to see what it was that was up there, but I was blinded by a sudden fluttering darkness.

The Maras were fleeing. They were pulling free from the sleeping Thors around us and running away.

One of them blew right through me, and a sudden rush of gratitude washed over me. I sensed the Mara's misery over its long imprisonment and forced labor there in the tower.

Then it was gone. They all were.

"What did we just set free?" Kara asked, and I blanched.

We had unleashed, if not demons, monsters with malicious appetites. My only hope was they would find few to harm so far in the north. And after feeding off the Thors for so long, I doubted they would feel their hunger again for a long, long time.

I had taken Reginleif's knife from the shadow man inside the dream, and it was in my hand as I stood up on the bed. I felt power within it. It was more than a mere blade. It felt to me almost like my wand did.

On impulse, I aimed it at the ceiling. I could see nothing, but I felt a dark dread descending down onto all of us.

Then it coalesced into an inky pool that dripped down to the floor.

Now it was more like a wax, congealing into the form of a person. I heard Thorfinna gasp and reach for her weapon, so I wasn't the only one who could see this being.

Then it lifted its head and looked at me. For a split-second, I thought it was Hulda. But this woman looked older. She still had a flickering effect where it was hard to pin down her age, this second in her forties, the next in her eighties, but the general impression was an older, heavier woman than Hulda.

Still, they could be sisters.

"Who are you?" I demanded, aiming my wand at her.

The woman smiled even as her form continued to take shape, her clothing gaining detail, her hair hanging loose behind her. Then she took a step towards me.

She opened her mouth as if to speak, but Mjolner was suddenly between her and me. His back arched impossibly high as he hissed at her.

The woman hissed back at the cat, then straightened back up to give us all a chagrined smile. "Sorry. That was childish of me. But I've always hated this one."

"Who are you?" I demanded, enunciating every syllable in case she had misunderstood me the first time.

"We've met before," she said, her eyes staring challengingly into mine.

For some bizarre reason, as my mind tried to place her, all I could summon up was the gray waves of Lake Superior. The deep, cold waters of that lake that I both loved and, respectfully, feared a little bit.

"Halldis?" I ventured, and she laughed a mocking laugh.

"Hardly," she said. "Nor Hulda, either. That was your next guess, right? My useless little tool. Well, I'm sure you'll figure it out with time. You're clever enough. For now, I'll say congratulations."

"For what?" I asked.

"For winning this little battle," she said, sweeping her arms over the sleeping Thors. "I won't pretend this doesn't hurt. It does. But in the end, it's just one battle. It's not the war. And doing what you did, you spent an awful lot of what she gave you. Wasted, maybe. Well, you'll see."

Then her gaze fixed on the knife in my hand, pointing at her although we were several feet away from each other, and if it had wand-like abilities, I had no idea how to access them. She licked her lips slowly, as if considering her options. She even took a half-step towards me. But she stopped at once, looking down at Mjolner, still hissing warningly at her. I was about to demand a better answer when, in the blink of an eye, she was gone.

Gone through the door, apparently, as it now stood swinging wide open.

But she also appeared to have taken the blizzard with her. The clouds in the sky broke up with improbable rapidity, and the rising sun filled the slice of sky framed by that doorway. The snow that had accumulated on the doorstep started melting at once.

And then the Thors started waking. Frór first, sitting up with a loud yawn. Then Thorulv and Thormund, who looked at each other first in confusion.

I heard Kara cry out, but it was a happy sound, and I knew Thorge had opened his eyes.

"What's going on?" Thoralv asked in a voice slurred and thick from long disuse.

I dropped down to my knees and grabbed Thorbjorn's shoulders to shake him desperately. For a moment, I thought I had lost him. That my nemesis, whoever she had been, had allowed the other five to go free but kept my Thor as her personal prize.

"Stop," Thorbjorn objected, swatting at me weakly even before his eyes cracked open. "Ingrid?"

"Yes," I said, letting him go. "It's me. I've found you."

He blinked up at me, then said, "well, it's about time."

"That's how you say thank you?" I said. "We went through a lot to get here. A lot! And then—"

But I didn't get to finish, because Thorbjorn had sat up and was crushing me in one of his bear hugs. I could probably have tried to keep talking, but it would've all been muffled against his chest, so why bother?

But as much as I had longed for that hug, and as good as it felt, it also made me sad. I could feel how weak he had become. His chest was hollow somehow, and his arms were thinner.

How long had he suffered? While I was partying with my Runde friends and vacationing with my grandmother in the cabin on the lake?

"It's all right, Ingrid," he said, as if sensing my thoughts. "It's going to be fine now. I'm going to be just fine. But we should probably get out of here, just to be on the safe side."

"I know," I said, and he finally let me go.

The room around us had gone awkwardly silent, and my cheeks heated. Had that hug been too public a display? Not that I minded, but I was sure that Thorbjorn was going to get a lot of ribbing from his brothers for that show of emotion.

Then Thorbjorn chuckled under his breath, and I belatedly realized we weren't the ones making a show.

Thorge and Kara, sitting up on the bunk next to us, were very, very happy to see each other.

"I'm going to check on the animals," Thorfinna announced, far too loudly.

"I'll help you," Frór said, close on her heels. Mjolner was riding his shoulders just as he had in the nightmare.

The other three Thors followed a touch more slowly, and I knew that a ribbing was indeed coming, if directed at a different target.

"Come on," Thorbjorn said, taking my hand. "We should give them a moment."

"Right," I said, stopping only long enough to fetch my art bag from the floor by the bed before following him out the door.

The others were making their way across the chasm on the rope bridge that had miraculously survived the storm intact.

I slung my bag across my body and made sure all the pockets were zipped closed. All necessary tasks before crossing that bridge, but if

I'm being completely honest, they were also handy ways to avoid looking at Thorbjorn.

I could remember when Kara hadn't even known that Thorge had existed, not really. But they were clearly an item now. And she was going to be a volva someday. She had a lot of training waiting for her, training she had barely even started, but I knew that was the path before her. I didn't really have that much of a head start on her.

And Thorge would be her guardian. There was no question about that.

But that was supposed to be me and Thorbjorn. We had promised that to each other when we were kids.

Had we just been usurped? Because we were moving too slowly?

"I'm glad all that worked out," Thorbjorn said. I looked up at him, and he cocked a thumb back over his shoulder towards the door into the tower. Which was not making his meaning any clearer. "Kara and Thorge," he finally said.

"Oh, yes," I said, and I could feel my cheeks flushing. If only I knew a magical way to keep that from happening.

"It was awkward for me for a long time with Kara, but I'm going to like having her as a sister-in-law," he said.

"Well, that might not happen right away," I said. "She's discovered she has the potential to be a volva, and I think she intends to pursue it."

"A time-consuming calling," he said sagely. "But there's no hurry. In such things, there is never any reason to hurry. Everything has its season. Or so I've always thought."

"That takes a lot of patience," I said evenly.

"You know what takes patience?" he said, leaning close to whisper only to me. "Having to pretend not to notice that someone like Kara is attracted to you when you know you're not right for each other. How long did I have to wait?"

"For Thorge to get her attention?" I asked.

"Among other things," he said, and there was a sparkle in his green eyes. But then he nodded towards the rope bridge. "Our turn."

"Right," I said.

The second time across was no easier than the first, even without the rain and wind trying to pull me from the ropes. It only made the view below my feet that much clearer and more stomach-churning.

But Thorulv was waiting on the far side to give me a hand up, and then I was once more on solid ground.

"That's all I need. The rest is yours," Thorfinna said as she emerged from the back of her wagon.

"What do you mean?" I asked.

"Thorfinna is letting us take her wagon," Thormund said.

I wanted to object, but not with an audience. I caught Thorfinna's arm, and she obligingly let me draw her away from the others.

"Look, I don't think the Thors can walk all the way back, and there isn't enough room in Reginleif's wagon for all of them," she said.

The Thors *were* looking decidedly weak, but still. "We can't ask you to give us your horse and wagon," I said.

"You didn't ask. I'm giving," Thorfinna said, once more in her booming voice. She slung her pack higher onto her shoulders. To judge by the rattle, it mostly contained weapons. And maybe that spare shirt.

"We thank you, Thorfinna," Thormund said with a formal little bow.

"You bet you do," she said with a wink.

"Won't you come with us?" I blurted out.

For a moment, Thorfinna looked touched by my question. But then she just smiled and shook her head. "Villmark is no place for me, but my thanks. No, I'm off to wander the north, just as I've done for all these years and will for years more, I'm sure. But if you ever have need for me, you know where to find me."

Then she looked up and down the road, decided to go on further into the mountains, and started walking. A moment later, she disappeared around the first bend in the road.

Thorge and Kara had crossed the rope bridge at last, and we were all there together in the morning sun.

"Where are we heading?" Kara asked brightly. "Were we still going to find Hulda?"

"No," I said. "We need to get back to Villmark as quickly as we can. Somehow, I don't think that's going to be as hard as getting here was."

"I hope not," Kara said. "So that thing back there, that woman. She's the one who sent the shadow man to kill Reginleif. To prevent her from helping the Thors escape her trap?"

"It looks that way," I said. "But we thwarted her."

"Something tells me we're going to pay for that later," Kara said.

We exchanged a look, then without another word climbed up onto the wagons, she on Thorfinna's and me on Reginleif's.

I was sure she assumed I wanted to get back as soon as possible because the Thors looked so very weak, and that was certainly part of it.

But the other part of it was Thorbjorn's nightmare. It had echoed too many of my own fears. I didn't know how Maras worked, if the visions they tormented their victims with had any hint of prophecy to them.

But I didn't want to risk it. We had to get home.

The Thors split themselves up between the two wagons and climbed into the back. I doubted it would be long before sleep took them again. But they needed it. Proper, restful sleep. And food, as soon as we could find any.

To my surprise, Mjolner hopped up onto the driver's seat beside me with a soft meow, then settled himself neatly, tail wrapped around his six-toed paws. He looked up at me and winked slowly.

"Not riding with Frór?" I asked him.

He meowed in answer, then turned his attention to the road ahead of us.

I wondered what was down that road, the one Thorfinna had taken.

I wondered if I would ever have the chance to know.

But I clicked my tongue to get the ox moving, and slowly turned the wagon around, to head back the way we'd come.

CHAPTER TWENTY-FOUR

IT TOOK days to get back to Villmark, but only half the number of days
it had taken to get to that tower.

And I spent most of them alone on top of that wagon. Well, alone
with Mjolner.

It might have been too much time alone with my thoughts. But the
roads were so narrow that Kara and I had to drive the wagons one
after the other. Side by side we could almost carry on a conversation,
but single file it was impossible.

Not that Kara was alone. Most days, Thorge was up there with her.
He looked like he was doing a lot of sleeping sitting up, and more than
once I saw Kara snatch hold of his cloak to pull him upright again
before he could tumble down to the road below. But it was human
company.

Frór and the other Thors were recovering, but painfully slowly.
Kara hunted as much as she could, and I figured out ways to prepare
all the staples Reginleif had left in her kitchen, but it never seemed to
be enough to fill in their cheeks.

"I'll go into town when we get back," I said to Thorbjorn one night
by the campfire.

"Go into town?" he asked. "We'll be *in* town."

"I meant into Runde, or maybe further, like to Grand Marais," I told him.

"For what?"

"Protein powder," I said. "And vitamins. Maybe even some of... what's that drink called? Provide or Guarantee or something."

"For what?" he asked again. He sounded amused.

"To fatten you up," I said. "Or bulk your muscles back up."

"Do I really look that bad?" he asked, lifting his arms and looking at them in the flickering firelight.

"You all look really thin," I said. My voice caught a little, but he pretended like he didn't notice it.

"We'll be fine," he told me. "Once we're home, and we're nearly there, we'll be fine. Trust me, my mother knows more about fattening the five of us up than you could even imagine. Or, as you said, bulking up."

I hoped he was right about that. I wanted to have a hug from him that didn't mix comfort at his warmth with feeling sad inside.

Finally, the day came when I started recognizing the hills and forests around us. We were nearly there. We had circled around further to the west than I would've thought. It would've been closer to take the five of them to their family's hunting lodge, but I was sure everyone in Villmark was waiting. And we would be there by dark, even at ox and wagon speed.

I don't know how anyone knew we were coming. Maybe someone hunting or foraging in the woods had seen us without hailing us. But when we topped the last hill and rolled into the town itself, there were crowds gathering in the streets.

I knocked on the side of the wagon. "You guys probably want to come out," I called to them. "You've got a lot of people anxious to see you."

The door banged open, and one after another the Thors spilled out onto the road. After days of resting, they were strong enough to walk on their own, if no faster than the wagon was rolling. But they fell into step by the wheels and waved to their well-wishers.

We got to the center of town before everything ground to a halt.

The crowds were too thick to drive any further. Not that it mattered; everyone we wanted to see was there already, waiting for us. I saw the Thors clustering around their mother, smothering her in the center of a five-way hug. Their father was running up from the road that led to the ancestral fire.

I didn't see Roarr. I hoped that meant that he had taken the watch so Valki could see his sons.

I didn't see Nilda either. She must still be hunting for Hulda with Yngvildr.

I hopped down from the wagon and took the yoke off of the ox. For days and days he had plodded on, and only now, at the end of the long journey, did that ox give in to any sign of exhaustion. I rather thought it was about to fall to its knees. I didn't know much about livestock, but I was pretty sure that was a bad thing.

"Ingrid Torfudottir?" someone said. I didn't recognize the man, but he was dressed more like a Villmarker farmer than a Villmarker tradesperson.

"Yes?" I said, certain he needed me for some volva business. I tried my best not to sound as tired as I felt. Which was probably pretty close to as tired as that ox felt. I mustered up a smile.

"Your animal, would you allow me to take care of it for you? You have a lot of people here eager to see you, but I don't think that poor animal should wait another moment to be tended to," he said.

"Oh, thank you," I said, blinking back tears of gratitude. "He's a good ox. Please give him extra treats. Whatever ox like."

He nodded and smiled, then led the ox away.

"I don't really belong here," Frór grumbled. Mjolner was purring in his arms as he petted the cat, almost as if not aware he was doing so.

"My grandmother would doubtless welcome the company at the cabin on the lake. That is, if you didn't want to go to your own place in the hamlet," I said.

"I think I need to see Nora," he said, blinking at me as if the thought had never occurred to him until I had spoken it out loud.

"Can you bring the wagon to her? She'll know what it means, I think," I said.

"I'll hire a fresh ox and take it at once," he said, and moved to hand me my cat.

"I wanted to ask you about something before you go," I said, and tried to draw him out of the crowd. It was actually easier than I thought. Once we were out of the square, the crowds were much sparser. But that made sense. It was densest closest to the Thors, who were already regaling the crowd with tales. But I was sure I had heard them all around the campfires over the last number of nights.

"What can I do for you, Ingrid Torfudottir?" Frór asked me once we were out of earshot of the others.

"I know all of you have said you don't know how you got into that tower or who was holding you there," I said.

He frowned at me. "I'm not sure I would describe it as a *who*," he said, not for the first time.

"Yes, but whoever—or whatever—it was, I think there was some connection between she—or it—and Halldis."

"Halldis, in the cell below us?" he asked. But he didn't dismiss me like I had feared he would. He just frowned thoughtfully.

"Halldis, but also… Hulda," I said.

Now he was scowling at me. "Don't speak that name near me."

"So you *do* know her," I said. "Did you two—"

"We're not discussing that," he said firmly.

"But she might be—" I started to say, but he didn't let me finish.

"She's… nothing. Nothing to worry about," he ended lamely.

"But that thing in the tower specifically mentioned her," I said. "And in her human form, she looked like both of them. Hulda and Halldis both."

"Well, that's hardly surprising," Frór said grumpily. But then didn't explain.

"I'm sorry, but why isn't that surprising?" I was forced to ask.

"Well, they all come from the same village," he said. Then quickly amended, "I mean, Hulda and Halldis come from the same village. I assume that thing is either a woman from there, or something that wants to look like a woman from there."

"From where?"

"One of the abandoned villages outside of Villmark," he said with a vague gesture towards the north and west. "If it ever had a name, it's lost to time now. But the women—and particularly the witchy women —from that town all looked like sisters. Across generations, all like sisters. I don't know how they were all related. But given the small population of the village, deeply entwined cousins might be the best way to describe it."

Deeply entwined cousins. What a nice way to say inbred.

"That's all it is?" I asked.

"That's all it is," he said with finality. But then he asked, "anything else?"

"Did you know Reginleif?" I asked.

A wistful look came across his face. "I knew your grandmother when she was a girl here in Villmark. But the first time I noticed her, really noticed her, was when I met her and Reginleif traveling together on that wagon over there. Not that I knew her well. But she and your grandmother were very close friends."

"After she died, I drew a sketch. It looked like purple coneflowers were growing out of her body," I said. "I thought that was a connection to Yngvildr, but the more I think about it, the less sense that makes."

"Hm," Frór said, and stroked at his beard. "I can't say for sure, but Reginleif had a look about her. She wasn't entirely Norse."

"Not entirely human," I nodded, agreeing.

"No," he said, then corrected himself. "Well, yes. Something else was going on there, too. But what I meant was, she was from Villmark originally. But long, long ago. I think she had some native blood in her."

"Ojibwe?" I guessed.

"Hm," he said again. "You have me wanting to check the Book of the Settlement. But if I remember correctly, her mother wasn't Norse or Ojibwe. There was another word. She came up from the south and married, or her husband went down to the south and brought her back. I don't recall which. Well, *you* could check the book."

"I will," I said. "So you're saying she was maybe Lakota or something like that? That makes more sense. It's a prairie plant. There's a lot more of it south of this state."

"Maybe that was it," he said. "If that's everything?"

I thought about the knife, still tucked away in my bag. The one that felt like a wand in my hand. But that wasn't something to talk to Frór about. That would have to wait until I was back with my grandmother.

"Yes, that's everything, thanks," I said. "Tell my grandmother I'll be up to see her as soon as I can."

"I have a feeling she already knows that, but I'll pass it along," he said. Then he went into one of the shops further down the road. I supposed to see about that ox.

I moved closer to the fringes of the crowd and saw Thorge and Kara standing on top of Thorfinna's wagon. Thorge was saying something I couldn't quite hear, but the deep, happy blush to Kara's cheeks told me enough.

They were engaged. Or engaged to be engaged, at least.

"Didn't see that coming, did you?" I heard Loke say. I turned to see him leaning against the wall behind me. In the shadows, of course.

"Believe me, if you'd been near them for the last few days, you'd've seen it," I said.

"Jealous?" he asked.

"Of Kara?" I asked. Then something had me blurting out, "I only ever was looking at Thorge because I want to draw his tattoos. Seriously, that's it. No attraction there."

"Woah, got it!" Loke said, holding up his hands as if to ward off my spew of words. "I meant the both of them, really."

"The last thing I want is to be the center of attention," I said.

"And yet you so often are," he said, and gave me that wide grin that was always so maddening.

I confess I had missed it.

A cheer roared through the crowd, and then the crowd started to break up, but not disperse. It looked like some were bringing in food, and others tables. It was about to turn into a proper party, despite the setting sun and the cool spring air.

I quickly stepped into the shadows to hide there with Loke.

"What's wrong?" he asked. "It's not like you to dodge away from a party."

I didn't know how to start this conversation. Aside from knowing what information to convey first, with Loke there was always the problem of controlling the tone. Because he would joke. And what was troubling me was no laughing matter.

"Do you remember what we were talking about? Before I left town?"

That did it. The grin melted away, and he said, "of course. But you brought the heroes home."

"I don't think that's going to be enough," I said. It wasn't all that cold, and I was still dressed for traveling in my coat and boots. But I shivered all the same.

"What happened out there?" he asked.

"A lot," I said with emphasis. "But the part that's plaguing my mind was more like a vision, I guess."

"A vision?" he said.

I chewed on my lip nervously. "I had to go into Thorbjorn's nightmare. To save him and the others from a nest of Maras."

"Maras don't *nest*," he said, but I was already waving his words away.

"It's a whole thing, forget about that bit," I said. "The thing is the nightmare that Thorbjorn and the others were trapped in? I can't shake it. It felt too real to me. It's like… that's the thing I was fearing. It's the thing I felt was about to happen here."

"Do you feel it now?" he asked.

I closed my eyes, but it didn't take long before I opened them again. "Yes."

"Yeah, me too," he said.

"What do you think it means?" I asked.

But before he could answer, a hand was closing on mine from behind me, and I was being pulled out of the shadows.

"We'll talk later," Loke said. That grin was back, but rather than joining the rest of the village at the party, he wandered off down an alley, taking the first turn possible so that he would vanish from sight.

"You're dancing with me, Ingrid Torfudottir," Thorbjorn said. I don't know if he had seen Loke there or not, but he seemed confused as to why I was dragging my feet about going back to the party.

The shouts and cheers of the crowd, especially since the ale was now flowing freely, were to my ears too much like the cries of that nightmare. The same voices. Just a little shift in the emotion. That was all.

"Ingrid?" Thorbjorn said, finally noticing my mood.

But I summoned up a smile. Thorbjorn, who never danced so far as I knew, was pulling me towards the music now. There was no way I was going to miss this opportunity.

Everything else could wait.

But that wasn't weird. Not for any of us.

I knew that Loke and I weren't the only ones feeling a strange foreboding in the air around Villmark. I didn't know who else felt it—and I would have to add that to my list of things to do—but I knew I wasn't alone.

But it wasn't weird. We descended from Vikings, all of us. And the one thing every Viking lives with, every day of their lives, is knowing how it's all going to end. We don't know when, but we know how.

Ragnarok was always coming.

But never arriving. Not yet.

And if I had anything to say about it, it wouldn't come for my friends and family. Not anytime soon.

I put my arms around Thorbjorn, and we danced the night away.

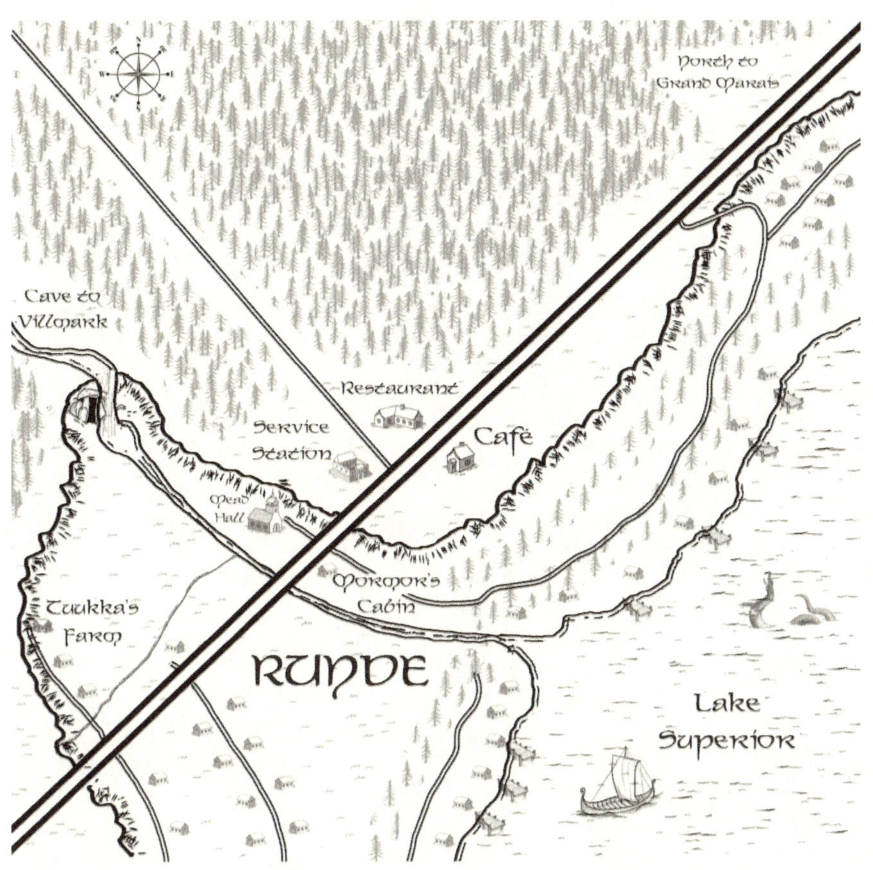

North to
Grand Marais
Cave to
Villmark
Restaurant
Service
Station
Café
Mead
Hall
Mormor's
Cabin
Tuukka's
Farm
RUNDE
Lake
Superior

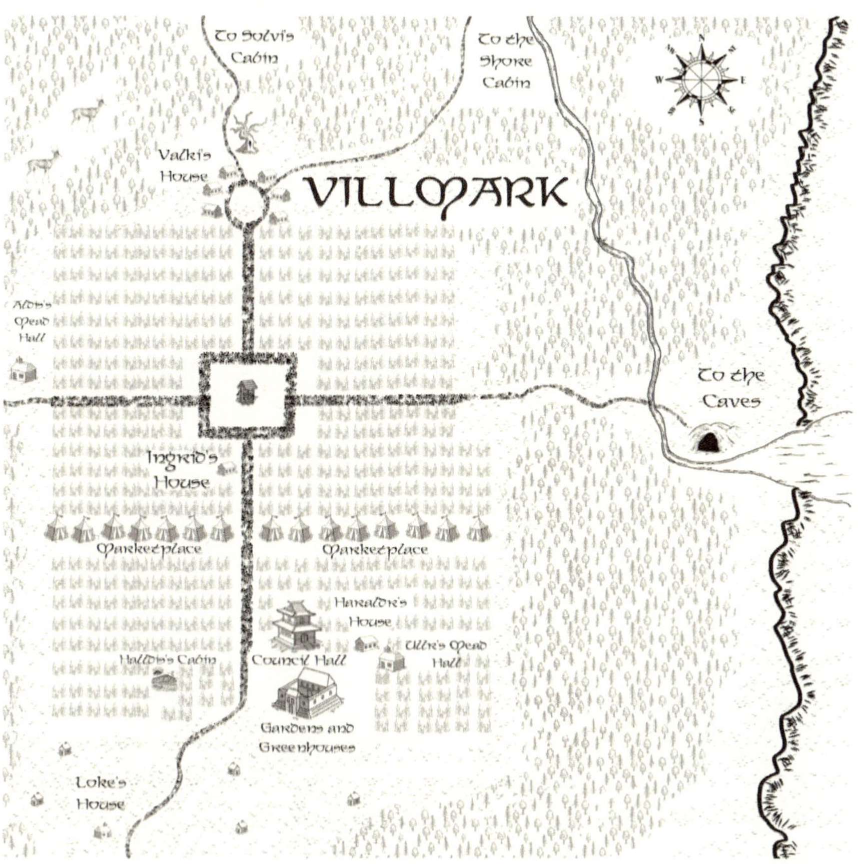

To Solvi's Cabin
To the Shore Cabin
Valki's House
VILLMARK
Alob's Mead Hall
To the Caves
Ingrid's House
Marketplace
Marketplace
Haraldr's House
Halldis's Cabin
Council Hall
Ullr's Mead Hall
Gardens and Greenhouses
Loke's House
N
S
E
W

CHECK OUT BOOK NINE!

The Viking Witch will return in **Sacrifice Behind the Falls**, available now!

Ingrid Torfudottir lives a double life. Half she spends in Runde, a normal town on the North Shore of Lake Superior in modern day Minnesota. The other half she spends in Villmark, a village that exists outside of time, where descendants of Vikings still live following the old ways.

On top of all that, she personally descends from a long line of volvas, women trained in the magical arts. Only she missed out on everything when she grew up away from Villmark. Now she still struggles to catch up.

After months of hard work, she speaks the language of Villmark. Her mastery of the runes sits at nearly a third complete. But now she must face her greatest challenge yet: the woman she narrowly defeated once before, who waits for their face-to-face confrontation deep inside the caves behind the waterfall that separates Runde from Villmark.

No one thinks she is ready for this rematch. Not her friends. Not her mentor. Not even her own grandmother.

No one but Ingrid.

Sacrifice Behind the Falls is book 9 in **The Viking Witch Mystery Series!**

THE WITCHES THREE
COZY MYSTERIES

In case you missed it, check out **Charm School**, the first book in the complete **Witches Three Cozy Mystery Series**!

Amanda Clarke thinks of herself as perfectly ordinary in every way. Just a small-town girl who serves breakfast all day in a little diner nestled next to the highway, nothing but dairy farms for miles around. She fits in there.

But then an old woman she never met dies, and Amanda was named in her will. Now Amanda packs a bag and heads to the big city, to Miss Zenobia Weekes' Charm School for Exceptional Young Ladies. And it's not in just any neighborhood. No, she finds herself on Summit Avenue in St. Paul, a street lined with gorgeous old houses, the former homes of lumber barons, railroad millionaires, even the writer F. Scott Fitzgerald. Why, Amanda can practically hear the jazz music still playing across the decades.

Scratch that. The music really, literally, still plays in the backyard of the charm school. Because the house stretches across time itself. Without a witch to protect this tear in the fabric of the world, anything can spill over. Like music.

Or like murder.

Charm School, the first book in the complete **Witches Three Cozy Mystery Series!**

THE WEAL & WOE BOOKSHOP
WITCH MYSTERIES

In case you missed it, check out **The Teashop Terror**, the first book in the complete **Weal & Woe Bookshop Witch Mystery Series**!

No one knows more about every branch of magic than Tabitha Greene. She devoted years to studying the most esoteric texts, hunting down the most obscure source materials, and deciphering the most cryptic ancient scrolls. But her career in academia hits a dead end when no wizard will take her on as an apprentice.

Just because, despite being descended from two long and prestigious lines of witches, her attempts to actually perform any magic always fail. Often spectacularly.

But no more college means no more dorm life. And no magical skills means no real job skills, at least, not in the witchy world. And a life spent moving from school to school every few months was a life without real friendships. She finds herself alone with nowhere to go.

Then an uncle she barely remembers offers her a summer job, running his bookstore over the summer. The Weal and Woe Bookstore, located in a magical pocket world within a block of buildings just north of the old Mill District of Minneapolis, Minnesota.

Not exactly the pinnacle of all her hopes and dreams. But it's just for one summer, right?

Or so Tabitha tells herself. But unbeknownst to her, the Weal and Woe Bookstore is about to change her life.

The Teashop Terror, the first book in the complete **Weal & Woe Bookshop Witch Mystery Series**!

The Ritchie and Fitz Sci-Fi Murder Mysteries starts with **Murder on the Intergalactic Railway**.

For Murdina Ritchie, acceptance at the Oymyakon Foreign Service Academy means one last chance at her dream of becoming a diplomat for the Union of Free Worlds. For Shackleton Fitz IV, it represents his last chance not to fail out of military service entirely.

Strange that fate should throw them together now, among the last group of students admitted after the start of the semester. They had once shared the strongest of friendships. But that all ended a long time ago.

But when an insufferable but politically important woman turns up murdered, the two agree to put their differences aside and work together to solve the case.

Because the murderer might strike again. But more importantly, solving a murder would just have to impress the dour colonel who clearly thinks neither of them belong at his academy.

Murder on the Intergalactic Railway, the first book in **The Ritchie**

and Fitz Sci-Fi Murder Mysteries, available everywhere books are sold.

FREE EBOOK!

Like exclusive, free content?

If you'd like to receive "A Collection of Witchy Prequels", a free collection of short story prequels to the Witches Three Cozy Mystery and Viking Witch Mystery series, as well as other free stories throughout the year, go to my website CateMartin.com to subscribe to my newsletter! This eBook is exclusively for newsletter subscribers and will never be sold in stores. Check it out!

ABOUT THE AUTHOR

Cate Martin has written stories which have appeared in **Mystery, Crime and Mayhem** quarterly magazine as well as in the annual **Holiday Spectacular** Advent calendar of Christmas stories. She is also the author of three witch mystery series: **The Witches Three Cozy Mysteries**, and **The Viking Witch Mysteries** and **The Weal and Woe Bookshop Witch Mysteries**. She currently lives in Minneapolis, Minnesota. You can learn more about her work at CateMartin.com.

Ashes Beneath the Tree (available July 14, 2026 direct from me or August 11, 2026 in stores everywhere)

The Viking Witch Mysteries Books 1-3

The Viking Witch Mysteries Books 4-6

The Viking Witch Mysteries Books 7-9

The Weal & Woe Bookshop Witch Mystery Series

The Teashop Terror

The Salon & Spa Scandal

The Bookseller Blunder

The Entrepreneur Enigma

The Novelty Shop Nightmare

The Courtyard Conundrum

Short Story Collections

Bubbly, Bicycles and Brides

The Dorothy Lundegaard Mysteries

Fruitcake, Festivities and Firelight

www.ingramcontent.com/pod-product-compliance
Lightning Source LLC
Chambersburg PA
CBHW020810190726
48285CB00006B/2227